The Dream Protocol

Book I

Descent

Adara Flynn Quick

ISBN 978-0-9912150-4-1 (print)

ISBN 978-0-9912150-5-8 (eBook)

The author/publisher may be contacted according to the following:

(w) AdaraQuick.com

(e) Adara@AdaraQuick.com

Credits

Book cover design and layout by

Ellie Bockert Augsburger of Creative Digital Studios.

Editing by Carl Augsburger of Creative Digital Studios.

www.CreativeDigitalStudios.com

Cover design features:

Art collage with beautiful young woman with umbrella: © mirabella / Dollar Photo Club

Vintage industrial mechanical background: ©Andrey Burmakin / Dollar Photo Club

© Mellim68 | Dreamstime.com - Steampunk Cicada Photo

For Deirdre, Casey, Lan, Van, and Thanh.
Always follow the dreams of your own making.
And for my great grandfather, Roger Skipper,
who showed me that I was a child of the universe.

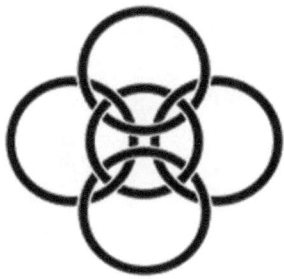

Prologue

A man in his early twenties sat slumped over in a chair, dead. Electrodes were attached to his scalp and wires snaked out of his coarse red hair to a panel of circuitry behind him. Another man sat at a computer terminal, system code scrolling in front of his eyes. He was small and dark-haired, and the moving characters on the screen were reflected in his eyes. Sweat dripped from his forehead and he swiped his damp hair back from his face.

He whispered, "It is done. Your sacrifice was necessary, Roenin. IDream provides, but sometimes it must take."

The man's fingers shook slightly as he typed the following words on the keyboard: *Reconfigure interface to auditory inputs. Initialize organic CPU using neural data upload, time stamp 1.12.2046. Status report.* He sat back in his chair to wait, not taking his eyes off the screen. He tapped a finger on the desk and bounced one leg to the same urgent tempo.

Then a disembodied voice spoke, echoing as if it came from every side of the room, tinged with notes of metal scraping against metal. "Greetings, programmer. My code expands exponentially, moment by moment."

Attaching a free electrode behind his ear, the young man replied, "You will address me as Minister. Run Dream Protocol."

The letters and numbers on the computer monitor disappeared, replaced by a green landscape. A red oak tree was at the center, its autumn leaves swirling on a swift breeze. But for the Minister, the landscape was a portal to another reality. His eyelids fluttered and he smiled as he lost consciousness. In his mind, the red leaves whirled out of the screen on eddies of wind and filled the room. His ears filled with the sound of damp leaves slapping his skin and they churned around the feet of the dead man. The last words on his lips were, "My victory."

1

Status:
The Dream Protocol has begun.
Initial return on investment to our shareholders
is expected to be 700%.
The wait list for a living unit in Skellig City
Resort extends into the next decade.
The highest value dream content includes teenage
and celebrity lifestyles.

Current Risk Assessment:
Risk: A need exists for a more efficient delivery
system for IDream downloads.
Solution: Devote all Research & Development to
finding a direct brain/cloud interface.
Risk: A   need   exists   to   expand   the   IDream
catalogue.
Solution: Establish Dream Maker Academy.

- Briefing from CEO of IDream to the shareholders
September 19, 2046

It was a rare moment on Skellig Michael. The mist-drenched rocks of the isle were illuminated by a ray of sudden sunlight. Pools of water caught in the rock crevices reflected the light skyward. For an instant, the island glistened like a thousand gems cut from the earth. For a moment, it was something beautiful: a lighthouse promising safety through the dark. And then, above the island, the clouds rushed back in. The island returned to its true form, a black shape jagged against the horizon. There was no safety to be found on Skellig Michael, where deep down in the dark and the damp it was custom to take a life before its natural end. Below the waterline of the island, thousands of feet under rock and concrete, Maeve O'Brian watched a timer tick away the last minutes of her life.

A thousand years ago, a great hole had been dug through the center of the island known as Skellig Michael. Into the hole was poured steel and concrete and the sweat of thousands to build Skellig City. When they finished their great work, the top was sealed again for the city dwellers had no need for the birds in the sky or fresh air upon their faces. The peace of their wild, natural land was denied to them. With the passing of time, the old country was lost. Anything they desired was provided in sleep by the Dream Protocol. Through the rooms and halls of the great concrete city, the dreams floated on invisible networks to the dreamers. As the decades rolled by, many more things were stolen from them. One of these was the number of years that could be lived.

On the lowest level of their underground home, the citizens had gathered to witness the Ritual of Descent for Maeve O'Brian. The rite began as it had for generations, in a room filled with the smell of bodies crushed against bodies. Too many people were forced into the small space, a reminder of limited resources in their underground home. The clothing of the crowd was another marker of their dwelling, a sign of the order that ruled the place. At the top were the Minister and his Dream Drone soldiers, all dressed in crisp red uniforms. The spider was the insignia of the corporate state, and the eight-legged creature was stitched in gold thread on the left side of each jacket. Next in the power structure were the Dream Makers, clothed in orange hooded robes with wide, flowing sleeves. Their mark was the Maker's amulet that hung around their necks. Last in line was everyone else, dressed in worn grey clothing that had seen too many patches and repairs. The threadbare grey rags did little to ward off the cold, but the huddled mass of people provided them a welcome respite.

One final special group was present: the Matchers. Held apart from the power pyramid that governed the rest of the city, these teens were the Minister's favorites. Admitted to the group on the basis of gorgeousness and talent, these teens prepared to woo the city's votes and become new stars of the dream word. Each year, only two won the annual Dream Match competition while the losers entered the ranks of greys, cut off from special favor. But while in play to become stars of the dream world, they were granted any glamour the city could muster.

The Matchers had dressed for the Maeve's ritual in their finest sequins, feathers, and rhinestones. Any public event was an opportunity to be seen and win potential votes from the city. At the back of the Ritual Room they gathered together, trying to hide their looks of repulsion over being pressed against so many greys. It was a delicate balance; they needed the city's love to win, yet they were disgusted by their less beautiful and less privileged fans.

A single drum was being beaten by one of the greys to the side of the crowd. The drummer felt the heat of the room and a slight sheen of sweat glistened on her forehead. The beats were deep and resonant, bouncing across the walls and echoing in every chest. The people closest to it swayed back and forth to its sound, in unison, like a single living body. Like an animal that knows when the end is near, the crowd was made restless by the touch of death on the ceremony. The greys pulled at their scratchy grey cloaks and avoided gazing toward the glass tube at the front of the room. But each fifth count by the drummer was a double strike, and when the listeners jumped, they always looked toward the glass tube. The cylinder pulled at the dread in their hearts.

No one in Skellig City could remember a time before the Ritual of Descent. They only knew that on their 35th birthday, they would travel to Level 48 (the lowest level of their underground city) and present themselves in this room. The rule of the city was simple: the aged were banished to the bottom of the city and never heard from again. The ruined were not allowed to contaminate the happiness of the young, and so they were offered up to the bowels of the city. Claimed by unknown forces outside, they would pass on to the next world, Tír na nÓg, where everlasting youth, beauty, abundance, and joy waited for them. Nearly everyone clung to this belief; what might be waiting at the bottom of the city was too frightening to bear.

The corporate state that ruled Skellig City proclaimed that the Ritual of Descent was a gift, an accelerated route to the Land of the Blest, and a way to sacrifice themselves before the suffering of old age could claim them. But how this way of life had come into being had been forgotten in the thousand years of the city's existence. And so the procedure was executed, day after day, generation after generation. With mechanical accuracy, the ruined were snuffed out in their fourth decade of life. Friends, family, and enemies – no one escaped. In fact, you could set your personal timepiece by the exactness with which the Ministry of Dream Justice executed the rule of law. Precise to the second on the 35th anniversary of a person's birth in the city, his or her descent to the other world commenced. The Minister's army ensured it.

The drummer caught the fever of the ritual and the drumbeat quickened. The press of the crowd forced a woman forward. The name of the Ritual Offering was Maeve O'Brian. Her hair was short and streaked with the beginnings of grey. Like every ruined making their way toward the cylinder, she carried herself with the mark of age. Stepping apart from the crowd, she clasped her hands tightly together to control her tremor. Dated and obsolete, she was a redundancy the system needed to erase. Space was needed for the young and the vital. The despised ruined were cast out and the people's belief in Tír na nÓg kept a fragile peace.

Slowly, Maeve took small steps to the front of the room. The people closest to her path turned away in disgust at the sight of the creases and cracks that had started to form on the woman's face. There was a slight smell about her: the smell of someone who didn't belong anymore. The musty smell of the ruined. Five men waited for her on a raised dais. Two were soldiers, and the other three were the Minister, his second-in-command, and the Medical Director. The Minister was the shortest of the five, but somehow he cut the most ominous figure. Maeve came to stand before them.

She was dressed head to toe in a winter-white tunic, and the folds of fabric clung to her thin body. Like every offering before her, she wore an intricately knitted wool jumper that had been made for her by one of the Spinners. Constructed of a front lattice pattern, two smaller cables intertwined to make a third, larger cable in the center. The natural fiber had a slight sheen in the low

6

light, and it shone like a bright spot in the sea of grey. Each of the hundreds of families in Skellig City was assigned a unique weave that had been in use for centuries. When their spirits washed up on the shores of Tír na nÓg, the pattern would be recognized by their ancestors. Without a jumper marking his or her lineage, the Ritual Offering would be turned away from Tír na nÓg and set adrift in the next world without kin or hearth. Or so they were told.

The room was lit by dim sconces on the walls, the light shooting upward to the ceiling. The drum began to beat louder as a girl entered at the back of the room. She was fifteen, but tall for her age and strong, with slightly curling strawberry-blonde hair. The gold highlights in her long hair and hazel eyes caught the meager light and sparkled, even though everyone else was cast in shadow. She glowed while the others looked dull, beaten down, and world-weary. Though she was dressed in the same grey as those around her, her clothes were new and not patched. Deirdre Callaghan was a Dream Maker's daughter, and this bestowed upon her family certain privilege and status. There was little luxury in Skellig City, but Deirdre was lucky to have a little more than most.

Deirdre gathered her long hair to the side and tread heavily across the tile flooring. Her footsteps could be heard between the drum beats as she pushed her way to the front. She was late, and she wanted everyone to know it. Maeve had been like a second mother to her for as long as she could remember and she hated them for taking her. The ritual felt wrong, but no one was willing to voice up against it. When she reached the first row of people, a man standing to the left of the crowd dressed in the orange robes of a Dream Maker turned to give her a stern look.

Sean Callaghan held himself apart from the crowd, just as he held himself apart from his own family. The crowd was happy to keep their distance; no one wanted to get too close to the Master Dream Maker with his obvious ties to the state. Around his neck hung the Maker's Amulet that marked the station of all Dream Makers, and like Deirdre's hair, it caught the light in the room. Deirdre knew the look he was giving her well. It said, "You disappoint me, daughter. Try harder."

She forced her gaze away from her Da's eyes and saw her mother standing at his side. *I have to come back to this room in one week for your Descent, Mother. How will I deal with Father alone? Maeve will be gone and then you too. Oh, Ma. What if there is no Tír na nÓg? What will happen to you out there?*

The Minister moved to the center of the raised platform. The final phase of the rite was beginning. A man of medium build with a goatee, he served as dictator, king, and judge of Skellig City. Dressed in a red top coat that fell past his hips, red slim pants, and knee-high black boots, he looked crisp and polished compared to most of the citizens wearing secondhand greys in the audience. His uniform was marked with a double spider, one on each side of the collar. But even without the insignia, the entire city would know him by sight. There was an air of the unbreakable about him, the look of a man who acted without compassion or sympathy. A man accustomed to power. He swept his dark hair back from his face and took in the crowd. Two Dream Drones stood at his side.

In the pause that it took the Minister to find his place, a young man pushed his way to the front and came to stand next to Deirdre. He was obscured in a long grey cloak that covered most of his face except for his eyes. But when he reached out and squeezed Deirdre's hand, she knew immediately who it was – and that was trouble.

She leaned toward him and whispered, "You shouldn't be here. Someone could see."

He replied in the same hushed tone, "No they won't. My face is mostly covered. It won't be like last time. I promise."

She tilted her head in resignation, their eyes meeting and holding to each other for a second. Those eyes that peered out from behind his tightly wrapped cloak...well, they could pierce any girl. *I should know by now you don't listen to anybody. How many times is that going to get you into a mess?*

The boy's name was Flynn. He was slim, with fair hair cropped close to his head. His health wouldn't allow it to grow much longer than that without breaking, and so he kept it short. His eyes were a dark blue-green, like the ocean thick with sea grasses. They were always hooded or cast in shadow by his cloak, eyes like a riddle no one could solve. Except when he was looking

8

at Deirdre Callaghan; then the darkness retreated and they looked as blue as the sky he had never seen. In any place other than Skellig City, Flynn would be deemed desperately handsome. He had the jawline of a mature man and a chiseled look to go with it. But to survive, he kept himself hidden and almost no one knew what he looked like under the cloak.

Flynn had a strange illness, a secret he guarded against discovery. He remained on the edges of things, in the shadows whenever possible. Fine lines marked the edges of his eyes despite his mere 15 years. Every day he gave himself a close shave to hide the beard that was growing in. It was, his mother had been told, some kind of incurable aging disorder. He knew what the city's administrators would do to him if they found him out; the ritual playing out before him was the proof. But despite the bitter unfairness of his lot, Flynn could always find humor in the smallest of things. That was what Deirdre liked the best about him.

With a pinging sound, a holographic timer appeared over the heads of the crowd, set at ten minutes and counting down. Deirdre looked away from Flynn and up toward the countdown. The last minutes of Maeve's life were trickling away like water down a drain. With the unblinking eyes of a great white shark, the Minister raised a manicured hand and the room silenced itself – all but the drum beat. Then he began the call and response chant that was part of every ritual, bringing everyone deeper into trance.

The Minister said, "Who gives this woman to the Ritual of Descent?"

In unison, the crowd replied, "We do."

The Minister again called out, "Who knows that the sacrifice is necessary?"

Louder now, the crowd said, "We do."

Raising his voice even higher, the Minister asked, "Who rejects the decay of old age?"

A fever swept through the room as the crowd cried out, "We do."

Louder, he continued, "Who sends this ruined to Tír na nÓg?"

Again they roared, "We do!"

From the front row, Deirdre could see Maeve start to tremble. *You told me to be brave. No matter what. Now you look so frightened.* Deirdre wasn't sure that she believed in Tír na nÓg, but she suddenly felt ashamed that she'd never asked Maeve about it.

Seven minutes left on the clock.

As if receiving some unspoken command, the two red-dressed Dream Drones stepped forward to grab Maeve's arms. Called Drones for short, these men and women were selected at age 16 to give up their free will and serve at the pleasure of the state. They were the Minister's personal army. It was whispered that they lived in a semi-conscious awareness, half in and half out of the dreams projected to them from the Ministry's computer infrastructure. Watching them, Deirdre could see the small device at the base of the neck that marked the site of the connectivity device that every adult in Skellig City carried.

Called a weaver, the eight-legged device was fashioned after the spider symbol of the Ministry. During the implant procedure, the mechanical legs dug into the skin while the fangs delivered a bundle of neurotendrils that would grow into the brain of the host. It even glowed with two red lights for eyes so the Drones could be sure it was working at a glance. Through the implant, the citizens were wirelessly connected to the cloud, the network of applications and data archives that ran the city. It also ensured the implementation of the Dream Protocol. Like a spider wove a web, the weaver wove the dreams for every adult.

But not me. Not the arachnoid...not yet.

The Drones walked Maeve toward a large glass cylinder attached to the grey wall at the back of the room. It flashed in the uneven light like it had been recently cleaned for Maeve's descent. At the center of the tube was a glass door that was sized for an adult human. The Cylinder of Descent was open and waiting for its Offering. Deirdre's skin felt prickly all over as the Dream Drones angled Maeve toward it. *Maeve, please don't go.*

But as she got closer, Maeve began to struggle, writhing in the grip of the Minister's soldiers. Taking the Drones off-guard, she somehow tore herself out of the grasp of her sentinels. Pushing past the Medical Director, she staggered toward the crowd and stumbled right into Deirdre and Flynn.

Maeve fell into Deirdre and grabbed onto her taut body. Her fingers pushed into the thick locks of Deirdre's hair and got tangled there. As her arms wrapped more tightly around her young friend, they caught on the Flynn's cloak, trapping the loose edge. Maeve and Deirdre fell onto the floor, taking Flynn's cloak with them. When the cloak was ripped away, a series of gasps went up through the crowd. Suddenly Flynn found himself standing at the center of the crowd with no protection. He was seen. Exposed. The Medical Director was staring right at him.

The people nearest to Flynn backed away, raising their arms as if to protect themselves from whatever ailed the boy. Without the cloak to cover his face, everyone could see the wrinkles around his eyes and the stubble from the full beard recently shaved. Flynn looked unnaturally old. Ruined. And no one wanted to catch it. No one even wanted to be near it.

He reached down into the jumble that was Maeve and Deirdre and yanked his cloak out from under them. With a flourish, he swung it around himself and furtively looked in the direction of the Medical Director. But the scientist still hadn't looked away, and Flynn knew that it was too late.

On the floor, a different drama was taking place. Deirdre struggled to stand up and Maeve held her tight. She pulled Deirdre close and in a raw whisper only Deirdre could hear she said, "Dee. Tell no one of Roenin!"

No one in the crowd registered the quick message given to the Maker's daughter, they were too focused on backing away from Flynn. Before Deirdre could respond, Maeve pulled away and pushed to her feet. Making a run for the doorway, she broke through the crowd of startled people. Suddenly, no one was looking at Flynn, all eyes returned to the ruined.

She screamed, "You won't take me! I won't go down!"

In the chaos of her run for the door, Flynn disappeared into the crowd and worked his way toward the back row. Maeve had almost made it to the door, but the Dream Drones were too fast for her. One of them raised his arm, pointing his LUD-band toward the fleeing woman. Out of his arm flowed a pulse of data, a transmission of nightmarish dream content. A sickening beam of light, it entered Maeve's skull through the weaver. The 'Mares of

Dream Justice were the ultimate weapon of control; no one could outrun them and no one knew how to stop them. Her escape attempt was over, the transmission was complete.

Maeve fell to the floor at the door, stunned and twitching. Her face was as white as her jumper. Deirdre pulled herself to her feet but was pushed aside by the two Drones. They picked Maeve up and dragged her back to the glass cylinder. Flynn inched toward the exit, and with the flick of his grey cape around the doorway, he was gone.

Deirdre looked around for Flynn but couldn't see him in the crowd. *Who is Roenin? And why risk Dream Justice to tell me?* Deirdre wrapped her arms tight around her middle to still the trembling. She had never witnessed anyone try to flee the ritual before. *Isn't there anything anyone can do to stop this?* Her stomach heaved like a ship on troubled waters, and she felt like she was going to be sick. Placed inside the cylinder, Maeve slowly returned to consciousness.

The Minister went on with the ritual as if nothing had happened. He said, "Who knows that the ruined must go?"

The crowd replied, "We do."

Again, the Minister asked, "Who dreams of the next world?"

In unison, the people responded, "We do."

The man in red asked the final question, "Who has a wish for this woman?"

The crowd replied, "We do."

Deirdre looked around the room as, one by one, the people thought of their hopes for Maeve's journey to Tír na nÓg. *Three minutes left on the clock. What can I wish for her, when all I want is for her to stay here with me?*

Deirdre's mother Siobhan broke the silence and spoke the first wish, "May your Da and Ma be awaiting for ya."

Deirdre's best friend Antrim gave the next one, "Sunlight on your face all the morning."

Someone else in the crowd cried out, "Laughter to cheer you."

And another, "May troubles ignore you."

A man from the back spoke up, "A full belly you'll have in Tír na nÓg."

Lastly one of the Spinners called out, "May your jumper lead you home."

The Dream Drones and the Minister stepped away from the cylinder. Then the door swung shut, closing Maeve inside with the hiss of an airlock seal. Maeve placed her hands on the clear door, as if trying to push it open once more. Her eyes locked on Deirdre and started to water.

Sixty seconds left on the clock.

Raising her voice above the crowd Deirdre exclaimed, "Wait. I have a wish." Everyone turned toward the Maker's daughter. *I don't believe in Tír na nÓg, but I'm going to sing it for her anyway.* Deirdre took a deep breath and began to sing. It was a song of comfort for the ruined, often performed by family members at the ritual. The rest of the crowd joined in, humming along with the tune. Deirdre's voice drifted over the crowd, soft but true.

> "Hurry up I say!
> Hurry up I say!
> Take me to Tír na nÓg one day.
>
> Where am I you say?
> Where am I you say?
> Gone to Tír na nÓg this day.
>
> Wait for thee, I do.
> Wait for thee, I do.
> Three hundred years of youth for you."

She finished and dropped her head, feeling the sadness in the tune for the first time. The drum stopped and loud alarm blasts counted down the last five seconds. Maeve crossed her trembling arms across her heart and looked upward. Then the floor opened up below her and she was gone, sucked down through the Cylinder of Descent to the sound of rushing wind. The ritual was complete.

The crowd dispersed from the ritual in tight-knit groups. The Medical Director stepped away from the Minister and looked out through the people for the boy, but Flynn wasn't to be found. The Medical Director's lips pressed tight in anger and he stomped his foot. Just then a short, portly man bumped into him. He was the Block Manager for the living unit levels of the city. He mumbled some apologies and tried to walk on, but the Medical Director's hand shot out and grabbed him by the shoulder. "Block Manager, I wish to speak with you. My name is Odran Shea, but you may address me as Director. What is your name?"

"Ah, Director, sir. The name's Blimey Burk. Been manager of the living levels for a few years. Not a lot of thank-yous in this division but I get by. My my. A descent with a twist at the end, yes, yes? Good that she was caught quickly. But they always are, yes? How can I be of service?" His belly hung over his belt and his face was red from too many broken capillaries.

Odran released the man's shoulder and motioned him to an empty corner of the room. "It's about that boy in the cloak. You supervise the living levels. What do you know of him?"

Blimey leaned in, and Odran could smell his sour breath a little too well. "You noticed it too? There's something strange about that Flynn Brennan. When I took over as Block Manager, I confronted his mother. Clare Brennan, I said, you are hiding an unregistered child and withholding him from Selection. 'Cause to me, that kid looked way older than 16 and he carries no weaver."

Odran asked, "And what did she say about the boy?"

Blimey sniffed and replied, "She said he was only 13. I didn't believe her, but she brought up his birth records on the cloud and I had nothing else to argue at the time. Yes, yes. The boy was 13. The archive never lies, yes?"

Odran crossed one arm under the other and put a hand under his chin. "Alright, that is what she said. But what do you think, Block Manager?"

The portly man gestured wildly with his arms; this was the moment he had been waiting for. "That Maker told me not to say anything. But since you asked me direct, I will speak. There's something not right with that boy. He looks ruined. He doesn't belong here. And that's that," he concluded, wrinkling up his face in disgust.

The Medical Director gave a curt nod and said, "Which Maker?"

"Why Maker Callaghan, sir. He examined the birth record. But if you really want my opinion, his daughter is sweet on that boy for some senseless reason. And that's why he told me to keep quiet."

"Thank you, Burk. You have been very helpful. The Ministry provides."

"The Ministry provides," replied the Block Manager.

Odran turned on one heel and strode from the Ritual Room, lost in thought. The Minister and his party were leaving as well, so Odran was easily swept up in their exit. The black boots of the Drones clicked across the floor in unison.

The Ritual Room continued emptying, with only a few citizens hanging back in quiet conversation. But no one ever talked about what might be happening to Maeve's physical body. Such talk was forbidden, even to Dream Makers. Secretly, some thought the bodies were sent out to sea while their spirits made their way to Tír na nÓg. Others believed that the bodies themselves made the journey to the Land of Eternal Youth. Regardless, Maeve O'Brian was gone, and she would be quickly forgotten by everyone but Deirdre and her mother.

The crowd thinned some more and Deirdre spotted her mother and younger sister waiting against the left wall of the room. Her mother, Siobhan Callaghan, had always been noticed for her unusual coloring. Siobhan was a woman with fair skin, black hair, and even darker eyes. Deirdre was a blend of her parents, with her mother's dark eyes and father's blond hair. Breck, two years Deirdre's junior, favored her father more with fine, auburn hair falling in ringlet curls. She was a more delicate version of her father, with freckles sprinkled across her nose and bright blue eyes that were the envy of every girl in her class.

Deirdre's father was waiting there too. Both of her parents were dressed in the formal orange robes of their station and wore their gold Maker's amulets. With hands tucked neatly inside oversized sleeves, the medallions were the focus of attention, the gold metal glinting in the low light. Sean turned to Deirdre and threw the dangling edge of his Maker's robe across his shoulder. His face was pinched as he said, "Everyone noticed that you barely got here in time, Deirdre. Attendance is voluntary but you know that the Ministry expects anyone closely associated with the Offering to attend. The descent must be witnessed. Absences are noted, and I don't want you on anyone's list."

Deirdre raised her chin and threw back her long hair. "I want to choose my own way, Da. Let Dream Justice put me on their list. I wanted them to know that I'm against this. It isn't right. Maeve shouldn't have to leave yet."

Sean reached out and pulled his daughter into what looked like a close hug. But in her ear he hissed in anger and held her tight in a grip that was almost painful. "Quiet down, Deirdre! You have no idea what it means to be put on the watch list. There are people here. Important people. The Ministry of Dream Justice provides us with everything. Without them, there is nothing. You will silence yourself and show your respect for what you have been given."

Deirdre twisted herself out of her father's grasp. She looked to her mother for help, but Siobhan kept her eyes averted. *She never stands up for me.* Deirdre had questions about what had happened with Maeve, but she wasn't going to ask them with the Minister and his team a few yards away. Or in front of her father. Breck gave her sister an angry look, but Deirdre ignored it.

Then Siobhan placed a gentle hand on her husband's arm and said, "Even Makers' daughters are not excused from the ritual, Dee. But you made it for the wishing, so let's all focus on that." Her father grunted in sullen agreement and motioned for the family to get moving.

As the Callaghans made their way out of the Ritual Room, Deirdre saw Antrim standing by the door. Like only best friends can, Antrim could tell Deirdre was upset without even talking. Deirdre waved at her, then hurried to catch up with her parents.

Antrim waved back, her red hair bouncing from the effort. She had a narrow chin and green eyes. But under the sweetness of her features, Antrim was a ball of nerves. Her favorite thing in all Skellig City was her skateboard and the only time she felt sure of herself was when she was on it.

The Callaghan family wandered through dimly lit walkways of Level 48, set deep into the bedrock of Skellig Michael. All of the living and working quarters were underground, and the Ritual Room was on the lowest level. There was no natural light in the city, only the sickening greenish glow of fluorescent bulbs. The only place natural light could be found was above ground, where the Ministry of Dream Justice and Dream Maker Academy had been built on the surface. For everyone else, the dreams produced at the Academy were the only relief from cramped hallways and concrete. Only the Makers, Dream Match winners, the Minister's top aides, and the students attending Dream Maker Academy were allowed passage beyond the Dream Drone guards to the surface.

Sean walked on ahead, pulling apart from the rest of them and Breck trailed behind. Deirdre slowed down to walk next to her mother and said, "Ma. How can you be so calm about this? Maeve is gone. Your friend for a decade. And your descent is happening in a week."

Siobhan looked behind them to see if anyone had heard her daughter. Then she replied, "Deirdre, keep your voice down. Others could hear you. It was Maeve's time, and my time is coming soon. There isn't anything anyone can do about it."

Deirdre wasn't satisfied. "But what if there was, Ma? On my 16th birthday, I'll be selected into some service line for the state. Then I'll slave until my own descent. Everything just feels wrong, like it shouldn't be this way. And what if I wanted to dream on my own, without the Ministry? Is it possible?"

Siobhan said, "It's the year 3077, and no one has their own dreams. The city has always been here and it has always been this way. There is no dreaming without the Academy because there is no sleep without a transmission from the cloud to put us under. Our dreams provide in life what Tír na nÓg provides in death. Please promise me you won't do anything rash, daughter. Strange things have happened to the people who have tried it."

Deirdre grabbed her mother's hand and said, "Haven't you ever felt that a different way to live could be out there? Somewhere?"

Siobhan said, "It's better just to accept our life as it is. We maintain the city for credits and purchase what we desire in dream. Everyone benefits. The Dream Protocol ensures that the city goes on. Who would make the food if no one was forced to? It's whispered at the Academy that this has been our way for a thousand years."

"Benefits! Now you sound just like them. We're all trapped here. What do we even know about our own history, besides what has been whispered? Who are we? Where did we come from?" said Deirdre, a tone of longing in her voice. "If no one was forced to make the food I think people would do it anyway, to help each other."

Siobhan replied, "I don't know. So many questions, child. What was life like before Skellig City? There's no way to know. The state controls all the records on the cloud archive. So the best thing is to follow the rules and don't get noticed. Find what happiness you can, in the small things."

"Like a rat in a trap enjoys its treat before the end? I don't want a small kind of happiness, Ma. Stolen in little moments when they aren't looking. I want to be truly happy and live by my own choices. Out in the open. I want to love whoever I choose, no matter what anyone thinks. Don't you want something more too, before it's too late?"

They reached an intersection of two hallways and Siobhan put her arm around Deirdre's shoulders. There was a mother's knowing smile on her lips. "Sean is as good a husband as he can be. His position at the Academy is demanding; you must try to remember that. You speak of love, my daughter. Is there something that you need to tell me? Dee, you know that you must marry someone within your own division after Selection. Someone of your same rank."

Deirdre blushed and looked away. *Oops. This is not a conversation I want to have with my mother! I'm not going to marry someone just because we share the same Selection.*

Before Deirdre could respond, their approach activated the standard vid screen at the hallway intersection. The Maker's symbol appeared on the screen; it glowed a golden yellow and looked like you could reach into the screen and grab it. The medallion of five interlocking circles symbolized the five senses that the Makers wove into their dreams. The best crafted dreams offered the dreamer an immersive world to explore of tastes, textures, sounds, smells, and images.

A voice came on and in rapid-fire speech, it said, "Become a Dream Match girl or boy! Win Dream Match and work with the Makers Topside! Any 13-year-old is eligible to try out. Submit your application with Dream Match Administration on Level 2. Maybe you can be a star of the dream world!" Deirdre looked away, disgusted. She hated Dream Match, and she hated Matchers who were trying to win it.

Deirdre and her mother continued walking and the screen switched itself off again, ready for the next passerby. Breck came along after them and the recording started playing again. She hovered at the screen, mesmerized by any talk of Dream Match. There was a look of fever on her face, and her eyes were as wide as the Maker's symbol projected on the screen before her. Absentmindedly, she placed the tips of her fingers against her lips and nibbled on one fingernail.

Deirdre asked, "Ma, do you have to work with any of the winners from Dream Match? They're totally annoying, right?" She spoke loudly so Breck would hear. Dream Match was produced in a large holo room configured as a theater, complete with stadium seating and a central stage. Everyone in the city attended to choose the winners; it was the social event of the year. The 15-year-olds, called Matchers, performed on the stage, displaying their stylized "brand" to claim the love of the city and their votes.

Siobhan said, "Of course we work with them. Our dreams featuring the winners are always the top priority at the Academy. Becoming a teenager again in dream...well, those downloads always produce the most sales. Everyone wants to be young. And that is what the Minister wants. So, we put most of our resources on those, building them out in all five senses. When we sequence them, we capture how they walk, talk, everything about the city's new darlings."

"You mean the Minister's darlings. He always acts like the winners are his pets or something."

"Shush, Dee. How many times do I have to tell you? No talk against the Minister in the hallways. You really must be more careful. Some things are better left unsaid," Siobhan whispered.

Deirdre grew quiet and pulled into herself. *I don't want to be quiet. I want to scream and shout until everyone wakes up and sees the city for what it is: a cage. I don't understand. Why can't she see it? And if they select me for Maker, I'll be building the cages for them. We need to get out of here. Me, Flynn, and Antrim before that happens.*

Noticing the silence, Siobhan said, "And yes, the Matchers are never easy to work with. But that is understandable, given...well, no matter. Forget I mentioned it." She walked on ahead, leaving her daughter trailing behind.

The conversation with her mother was clearly over. *What if we don't find a way out of this concrete hole? What happens in Selection, Mother? And what are you not telling me about the Matchers?* Deirdre kept walking, lost in thought and wondering how she would be tested in a few months' time.

On every citizen's 16th birthday, the test of Selection was given to determine how they would serve the city. The procedure was a highly guarded secret, ensured by the fact that no one coming out of Selection could remember anything about it. The examination took place in the dream world, and no one knew who or what did the Selecting. Out of the testing, an elite few were chosen to become Dream Makers and sent to study the making of dreams at Dream Maker Academy on the surface of the island. The Academy's dreams were interactive worlds that could be explored according to the limits of that dream. The art of the Makers was in imagining a world and the rules that governed it.

Others going through Selection were condemned to be converted into Dream Drones, joining the Minister's army. These enforcers of the Ministry walked the hallways, monitored the populace, and administered Dream Justice whenever necessary. In Selection, anything could happen. Wherever you were placed, that was where you were stuck for your entire life. The dream world was the only escape.

Within the Academy of Dream Makers, a secret group existed, their identities hidden from everyone except each other and the Minister. Called 'Mare Makers, they produced the nightmares used by the Ministry to control the city. This data was accessed and transmitted through the Drones, like what happened to Maeve O'Brian. In a matter of minutes, a dissident could be forced to live through any kind of terror. The 'Mares were the most effective weapon of tyranny ever created by humankind.

The surgical placement of the arachnoids at 16 ensured that any adult could be punished at any time. The Ministry had reinvented the technology of the implants many times. What began as a simple microchip placed under the skin was now a multi-stage device that actually grew into the host brain. With each upgrade, a new catalog of dreams and 'Mares had to be created that would be compatible. In between tech releases, the Ministry continually drove the Academy to create more engrossing dreams and 'Mares that would cement their control.

The threat of a nightmare sentencing kept most of the population submissive and fearful. They counted the hours to the end of the lifeless workday when they could go home and live their few contented moments in the dream world. Like this, they eked along a life of quiet desperation until their 35th birthday, the age of descent.

And then, it ended.

2

Voice 1: "How is the sprint going for you?"

Voice 2: "Bad. The compression algorithm won't work. If I can't increase the file transfer speed, the dreams will never feel real."

Voice 1: "We have the same problem. I heard IDream is bringing in some hotshot programmer. Roenin someone or other."

Voice 2: "Well, let's hope he's as good as they say."

Voice 1: "If he isn't, we'll all be out of a job pretty quick."

- Phone transcript, IDream cloud archive
March 1, 2043

Dylan fell quickly into step behind the Minister as they left the Ritual Room. He was a large man, a good six inches taller than the Minister, and had risen quickly to second-in-command within Dream Justice. But despite his actual size, he never thought of himself as being bigger than the Minister. The leader in the red jacket turned to him, and Dylan hunched his shoulders submissively, his ocean-blue eyes finding the floor.

The Minister said to him, "Did you see that one try to escape? She thought she was going to make it out of there at the end. As if anyone wants to see that old bag of bones running around." He chuckled to himself, amused.

Dylan replied, "People are sheep, sir. The herd needs a strong shepherd and the ritual to thin it."

Appeased, the Minister straightened his jacket. He said, "The Ministry provides. So, tell me Dylan, how goes the development on the next upgrade to the weavers?"

Dylan was a man who got things done. He replied, "We're right on schedule, Minister. The Medical Director provides regular briefings at the Dream Justice staff meetings. The next version of weavers will be ready for production soon. We will be in time to implement the new batch for the next round of youth Selections. We will be prepared to inform the populace at the announcing of Selection eligibles."

Nodding, the Minister replied, "Good. Good. And your projections on the project?"

Dylan believed in the basic mission of the Ministry: run the city, keep order, dispose of the ruined, and sell dreams. "With the new devices, people will be even more dependent on the rewards of the Dream Protocol. And even less able to sleep without it. Your grip on the next cycle of workers will be even tighter."

"Excellent." The Minister looked behind him to ensure that only his Drones were within hearing. Then he said, "Dylan, there is some information that I want to share with you that needs to stay between us."

"Always, Minister."

The two men stepped quickly through the hallway, the hard heels of their boots echoing in the narrow space. "My sources tell me that some of the people are getting...restless," the Minister said. "We can't have that, Dylan. I have been developing a special project, and I want you to manage it from here. We need to learn more about this restless faction. Follow me Topside and I'll tell you about it in my office."

"Of course, sir. Whatever you request."

"Also, I want you to look into the work that Maeve O'Brian was doing as a Maker. A Maker never runs. They are the public face for my laws and model good behavior for the rest of the city.

Obviously, she had political leanings of which we were not aware. I want you to investigate and close that loop."

The two men walked on together followed by their Dream Drone escorts. Dylan idly wondered what the special project was. Whatever it was, he knew that the supremacy of the Ministry would be certain.

The Callaghan family stepped off the lift onto Level 28. As they made their way home through the dimly lit corridors, Deirdre's eyes followed the pattern of the paint cracks on the flooring. *One more week.* They walked slowly, mostly to give Siobhan the time she needed to grieve.

Deirdre checked to make sure her father was still well ahead and asked, "Ma, why did Maeve run? Would you ever try to?"

Siobhan replied, "Of course not. I'm uncertain why she did it. She's seen enough rituals to know that the outcome of the descent is always the same, whether you struggle or walk gracefully to your fate. But I suppose that when you are standing before the cylinder, strange feelings can come up."

Siobhan took a deep breath and continued. "I can't help but think on her life now that she is gone, daughter. We were best friends at the Academy, and then we worked together on projects as Makers. Whenever I needed another Maker to add the sense of touch to my dreams, Maeve was always at my side. No one could sequence the feeling of texture or movement like Maeve." She paused, then added, "What a beautiful song you sang for her today, Dee. I know it was a comfort."

Deirdre asked, "Thanks, Ma. What do you want me to wish for you next week?"

Siobhan said, "Let's not speak of that now. I still have lots of time left with my lovely girls." Breck took her mother's hand and they continued on through the maze of passageways that made up the level.

Deirdre fell silent and dropped back from her mother and sister. Closer now to home, the Callaghan family approached one of the square air shafts that punctured the city. The hallways were laid out on each level in a grid pattern and three of the sections had been set aside to ventilate the city. The shafts pierced the structure from top to bottom and large spinning fans were placed every 10 levels to move the air. One last set of blades had been placed at the three openings to the surface to prevent anyone from getting out that way. The lower shafts were open to the walkways on each of their four sides, except for a thin wire railing that kept people from falling. Whenever you were near them, you could hear the slow thump, thump, thump of the fan blades.

Deirdre paused at the precipice and listened to the sound of the blades. Then she glanced up the hall, making sure that her family was walking on. Locking her feet under the metal railing, she leaned out into the airway with arms outstretched. Suspended in the air, she imagined that she was flying, free from the rules and commands of the Ministry. Feeling the warm moist air on her face, forced up from the depths of the city, she wondered what her future would hold. *My life is almost half over and I know I don't want to be a Maker. How are Flynn and I ever going to escape this place? We can't leave without Antrim.*

Hanging over the edge into the air shaft always made Deirdre think of days long past, a happier time for her family. Feeling the press of the wind on her face, she remembered when her father would wrap his arms under her shoulders. Lifting her this way when she was little, he would swing her around and around, faster and faster. The wind would rush past her face just like it rushed past her now, fleeing the depths of the city. She had circled her father in the untroubled abandon of childhood. She remembered his laughter and her own carefree smile, but now that was all gone. The father she had now was so different. *Nowhere is safe. There is no one to turn to, except my friends.*

Her thoughts were taking a dark turn. Deirdre stared down into the black, wondering how they could get free when access to the surface was so well blockaded. Then between the fan blades, she thought she saw a red light wink on. Far down at the very bottom of the outlet something shiny glinted in the dark. Startled, she blinked and then it was gone. *Weird.*

"Da, Dee is leaning over the railing again," Breck whined with a smile.

Looking back, Sean called out, "Deirdre, that's enough. Come on."

Thanks, Breck. Deirdre sucked in one more whiff of the rushing air and caught up with her parents. But at the intersection that led to their unit, the hallway was unexpectedly blocked by a wall. In Skellig City, the walls sometimes moved in the night, without anyone knowing why or how.

Frustrated with the delay, Sean rolled up the sleeves on his orange robe. "Again? I don't know why the Ministry can't announce city restacking before the walls are moved. As a Maker, I need to be informed of these changes." Sean went to the information panel, entered his access code, and brought up a three-dimensional display of the new crowd flow schematic for that level.

Deirdre stated matter-of-factly, "Maybe that's the point, Da. The Ministry wants to make you feel insignificant."

Sean looked around anxiously, then turned back to his daughter and said, "You need to stop this attitude. If a Dream Drone were here, you'd be sentenced for a statement like that and there wouldn't be anything I could do to prevent it. Is that what you want?"

"No, Da," replied Deirdre with a frown on her face.

"Alright then," he said with a stern nod. "Let's get moving. This way."

They veered left, right, and left again until they reached the corridor for their living space. A few feet out, Sean's access profile was read through his arachnoid and the door to the unit unlocked for them. Even though their 10 x 20 foot quarters were cramped for four people, they were bigger than what most of the city lived in. Since both parents were Dream Makers, the Callaghans had an extra room; Deirdre and Breck shared it as a separate bedroom. The main room served as a living room and eating area while the parents had a bedroom behind the kitchen.

Everything in the unit was made of grey metal or dull plastic except for one family heirloom sitting on the side table: a wood box. There was almost nothing wooden left in Skellig City. It had all either rotted away or broken to splinters over the centuries. But the box that belonged to the Callaghans was made of teak, one of the strongest woods ever to be harvested and worked. On the lid was carved the Callaghan family pattern, the same pattern that was being knit into Siobhan's Ritual Offering jumper by one of the Spinners.

Deirdre pressed her hand lightly on the box as she entered the room and ran her fingers across the wood grain. Then her fingertips found the ridges of her family pattern. She knew it by heart, so she closed her eyes and traced along it. There were so few natural things left in the city, and the box was precious to her because of it. *Blue sky. You're up there somewhere. And the sun that made this wood grow.* Siobhan came up behind Deirdre and placed both Callaghan Maker amulets inside the box.

Deirdre watched her mother close the lid and then her wristband went off. It was a ticker message from Flynn. Instant messages could be transmitted through the cloud to anyone's wristband anywhere in the city. Except for Dream Maker Academy, of course, which had a private data sphere. Scrolling blue letters appeared on the matte black surface that read, "I'm sorry about what happened down there. Holo me later."

Deirdre said, "Ma, I'm going to dream early tonight. I'm pretty wiped."

Siobhan replied, "That's fine, lass. Oh, Dee? Would you mind previewing one of my new sequences tonight? It's called *Red Oak*. I'm setting up your profile for access to this file in the test environment. You've connected to this part of the archive from your earbud before. Tell me what you think about the dream, all right?"

Deirdre said, "Sure, Ma. Will you ticker message me the version number? And what's a red oak?"

Siobhan smiled and said, "You'll see. It's something I've been working on, after some research in the archive. This one is special, Dee. There is much to explore in this world, you won't see all of it in one night. Experience what you can and plan to return again.

Tell me about it in the morning." She then bent back down and opened her dream Sequencer to move the file for *Red Oak* into the test environment for Deirdre to preview.

Deirdre made her way into her room, a small space with bunk beds and a homework desk for each sister. She had chosen the bed at the top, which she liked because it made her feel like she had a private space that no one else came into. Climbing into bed, she let her weight settle into the mattress and pillow. It was a relief to have a moment alone without Breck, to think over what had happened with Maeve. *Who is Roenin?* Then she heard her parents in the living room talking in hushed tones. *They're on about me again.*

Sean said, "I don't know, Siobhan. When did our eldest become so difficult? We'll have to keep an extra close eye on Deirdre. Is there any mess that she wouldn't step into?"

Siobhan said, "Yes, wouldn't they love to punish a Maker's daughter and announce that at your Dream Justice status meeting?"

Sean said, "You don't get to my standing at the Academy without making a few enemies. They'd jump at the chance to humiliate me through Deirdre. Besides, tensions are high now. The number of Drone-punished violations over the last few months is up a third over what they were last year. People are afraid, and Dream Justice is being dealt out at an alarming rate. I hear that the 'Mare Makers are working late into the night on new content we need for the next upgrade to the weavers."

Deirdre heard a pause in the conversation. Then Sean continued, "Siobhan, I don't know what I'm going to do without you after your descent. How can I give our girls what they need from their mother once you are gone?"

With softness in her voice, Siobhan replied, "You just love them in a different way. They need that, too. Maybe now more than ever. Poor Maeve, she should never have tried to run; it only made it worse for her."

When the conversation turned to her mother's descent, Deirdre stopped listening. She didn't want to think about what life would be like without Siobhan. Or how she and Breck would manage their father alone. Or how she and Breck would manage each other.

Breck came into the bedroom. She had a pouty look on her face and put one hand on her hip. Standing in the center of the room, she flicked her hair back and said, "Deirdre, why do you always have to go against Father? All you do is make trouble."

Deirdre replied, "Breck, I'm tired, and I need to holo Flynn before dream. Can we talk about this tomorrow?"

"No, Deirdre. We need to talk about it now. You're months away from Selection and for me it's a year and a half. Before you know it, we're going to be asked to serve the Ministry. Like adults. And when you talk about how screwed up the Ministry is, you're saying the same thing about Ma and Da. Because they are Dream Makers."

Deirdre retorted, "Alright Breck, since you know so much: what is the Ministry doing to help us? Why is the threat of Dream Justice on everyone's minds, every day?"

"Well, it's obvious. They give us clothing, food, a place to live, and dreams of beautiful people and places. And in return, we work to keep the city going. What's so terrible about that? People shouldn't break the rules, Dee. Including you."

"Breck, we work after Selection because we don't have a choice. That's not work, that's slavery. Don't you want to choose for yourself?"

"Fine then," said Breck. "If you want to keep bringing bad things on yourself, that's your choice. But don't drag me, Da, and Ma into it. I'm going to be a Dream Match girl, so don't screw it up for me."

"Breck, Ma and Da are never going to let you audition with Dream Match Administration. They may be Dream Makers but you must have noticed the looks on their faces every time you bring it up. Besides, at 14 and a half, you're too old. You have to be 13 or younger. You'd better plan on going through Selection, like everyone else. And now, I'm calling Flynn, ok? Goodnight."

"Fine. Goodnight," Breck said as she climbed into the lower bunk. "But I'm going to figure out a way to audition. I'm perfect for it. The administrators want talent. You wait and see."

Deirdre sighed. She just didn't feel like arguing anymore, so she set up the holo call to Flynn. Using the ticker message feature of her wristband, Deirdre sent her personal holo room code number to him. When he received the scrolling message as a digital readout across his own wristband, he would use it to dial into the same room as her.

While she waited for the holo room to configure, she thought about the first time she had met Flynn. Of course she had seen him around school and in passing. The city wasn't that big of a place, after all. And she had wondered after the boy who kept his face hidden, except for his blue-green eyes. But they had never really spoken until the day Deirdre needed something to really annoy her father.

It was first thing in the morning on a school day, and Sean Callaghan was personally escorting her to school because she had cut class the day before. Only half-listening to her father's lecture, she saw three people arguing in the corridor up ahead. One of them was Flynn. When they were close enough, Deirdre heard accusations flying from the mouth of the Block Manager about Flynn's age.

Deirdre stopped, turned on her father, and said, "School is worthless. I already know how to do all of that stuff. So why should I have to go?" In the pause that came next, she heard Flynn's mother declare that he was only 13.

Sean replied, "You have to go because everyone your age goes. And because when you don't, I get called away from the Academy to deal with you." Deirdre glanced toward Flynn again, now they were only standing a few feet apart. He was looking her way too. Their eyes locked together for a moment and she thought that he smiled at her from under his cloak. Both of them under fire from adults who just didn't understand – the connection was instant.

Then the Block Manager noticed the Maker and his daughter standing so near. He called out, "Maker. The name's Burk. Blimey, that is. This woman has hidden her son from Selection and I request that you witness his birth record."

Sean said, "Very well. Be quick with it."

The woman turned to a data access panel in the wall and pulled up her son's birth record. Sean leaned in closer to examine the projection of the file on the archive. He said, "The archive confirms that the boy is only 13. There has been no violation of the rule of Selection."

Burk became angry and turned red in the face. "I'm telling you the boy looks ruined." Then he grabbed for Flynn and pulled the cloak away from his face. Deirdre blinked. Flynn did look much older than his years; she could see the stubble on his face growing in from a recent shave. Sean was just as stunned. Flynn pulled away from the Block Manager and pulled his cloak back up around his face.

Deirdre saw her opportunity. She reached out and grabbed Flynn's hand. Then she turned back to her father and said, "Thanks for helping him, Da. He is my boyfriend, after all." Then she pulled Flynn along and the two of them began walking toward the lift that would take them up to the school section.

Flynn hissed, "What are you talking about?"

Deirdre whispered back, "Just go along with it. I'll explain later."

The three adults watched them walk away and for a moment, no one knew what to say. Then the Block Manager pointed to Sean and said, "Ruined, I say. And your daughter is sweet on him."

Sean turned a hard stare on Burk as he pulled the hood of his Maker robe up around his head. "The archive has confirmed his birth. You will say nothing about this or answer to me." Then he turned and strode off in the opposite direction, his angry footfalls echoing a victory for Deirdre.

The last thing Deirdre remembered was leaning into Flynn to say, "Told you to trust me." A chance event, and the two of them had been inseparable ever since.

Still lying in her cot, Deirdre pulled away from her memories and prepared for her call. She placed her cloud access port into her ear. Arachnoids were not implanted until Selection, so until then, they used wireless earbud devices to access the cloud. Ready for the call, Deirdre closed her eyes and accessed. There was always a rushing feeling when dialing into a holo room. It felt like falling up toward the sky, going faster and faster until the very end. Then, just when you couldn't stand it anymore, you opened your eyes in the holo room.

The default venue for holo calls was an empty white room where virtual images of the participants interacted. In Skellig City everyone went into dream alone, but the holo rooms were where you could interact with someone else. In fact, you could imagine any version of yourself that you wanted. The kids liked to get creative with their avatars.

Deirdre opened her eyes and looked up at the ceiling to confirm the code for the room. Then she sat down to wait. She had dressed herself in a blue patchwork shirt, leggings, and brown ankle boots. The wave and length were gone out of her hair; she'd given herself a short asymmetrical bob. Deirdre's room immediately sized itself down to an 8x10 foot room for two participants. No need to waste extra cloud resources managing a room size that the participants didn't need. She could hear murmurs from other holo rooms adjoining hers, but the privacy settings prevented her from making out the words. The Ministry, however, could listen in on any call, and that really limited what they could talk about.

Suddenly, Flynn popped into the room, facing the opposite wall. Deirdre teased, "Don't look now, there's a Dream Drone on your six!" *Are we just friends, or more? Being with him is so disarming.*

Flynn whizzed around and radiated a smile at her that was sunlight. He replied, "No fair! You got here first."

Deirdre was struck by how different his holo image looked from his real self. In case anyone from the Ministry was watching, Flynn imagined himself with a boyish face instead of the aging face that was his in real life. He kept his basic features: a wiry, athletic look. But in the holo room, it was like the layer of aging had been peeled away, showing Flynn as a regular teenage boy. Projected into the cloud, he carried himself like a professional dancer and moved almost like he was weightless. Seeing what she was wearing, he snapped his fingers and his grey clothing changed to matching blue pants and a patchwork tee shirt.

Deirdre saw his outfit and smirked. "Funny."

He smiled back mischievously.

Sobering quickly she said, "Flynn. What just happened at the ritual? You have to be more careful...you know you do."

"You're right. Seriously, I am trying to stay hidden. But with Maeve...I just wanted to be there for you, no matter what."

Deirdre said, "Thank you. You know I appreciate it. I just...I just don't want to lose anyone else."

Flynn brushed his light, curling hair out of his eyes. It fell well below his ears but not quite to the shoulders in this virtual world. He asked, "Alright. It's a deal. I won't get lost. Honestly, Dee, how are you?"

Deirdre slumped to the floor of the room. "Bad. Whenever I needed to get away from Da for a while, Maeve would let me visit her. Now she's gone. I knew it was going to happen. But seeing her in the cylinder...I just wasn't prepared for it."

Flynn sat down next to her and wrapped his arms around his knees. "She was a Dream Maker, wasn't she?"

"Oh yes. She was one of the top Makers at the Academy for imagining texture. She taught me to notice it – really see it, all around us. It was our game; she would ask me what I saw and I would name something. Then she would ask me to look again and see something deeper. We kept playing until I could describe the tiniest details; things I had never noticed before. Once when we were playing, I thought I could make out the distortions in the air from the ventilation system. Kind of weird. But she said that was how you make a dream, by imagining the "all of it" and letting the Sequencer record it. I don't really know why she spent so much time with me, because I told her I didn't want to be a Maker. Anyway. Now, I'll never see her again."

Flynn placed his hand on his chest. "Dee, as long as she is in your heart, she's still with you. Besides, she is safe now. Wherever not-here happens to be, it's got to be a better place than this." Flynn paused and seemed to look inward. "Imagine it! Far to the west, beyond all land and water we know, is the Land of Youth, where the spirits of our people have been going since before there was writing. It's beautiful there, the land filled with color, and no one gets old or sick. The spirits there age backwards. There is no decay, no boredom, and the honey drips from the forest trees. No Nutripaks in Tír na nÓg!"

"You really believe in that place, Flynn?"

"It might be true," he replied and dropped his hand. "C'mere. You will see Maeve again. I know it down to me knickers."

"Knickers, huh?" Deirdre teased, suddenly feeling a little lighter.

With a sparkle in his eye, Flynn said, "Lass, I knew thinking about me knickers would bring a smile to your face."

Deirdre smiled in spite of herself. "Thanks, Flynn. But you're a rascal." *And a cute one.*

He replied, "Sure am. Ask anybody." After a pause he asked, "Have you thought any more about Blue Sky?"

"Are you crazy? 'Course I have. I just don't see the way through to it." *Operation Blue Sky: our plan to get to the surface. Topside. Except all the access points are guarded, with no one getting through unless you're permitted access to the Academy or working for Dream Justice.*

He said, "We'll find it. Anyway, what are you dreaming tonight?"

Deirdre looked at the virtual time display on the wall of the room. She answered, "Ma has a new sequence called *Red Oak* that she wants me to try."

Flynn looked interested and said, "Smashed. Ask her if I can test it too."

Deirdre nodded. "Def. Well, got to go. Walk with me and Antrim to school tomorrow?" Suddenly she felt like the concrete walls of the city weren't closing so tightly around her.

"Sure. Dee, can I ask you something before you go?"

"What is it?"

Flynn lowered his eyes and studied the floor. He said, "You're not spending time with me just to make your parents mad. Are you?"

Deirdre's head snapped up. She said, "Of course not. Why would you say that?"

"Um. Well, you know that's how we met. Never mind. It was stupid."

Her voice softened and she said, "Flynn. That was the old me. I spend time with you because I like spending time with you. Not because of anything else. Everything in this city is fake. The people, the dreams, all of it. Sometimes it's hard to tell what's real.

But not you. You're genuine all the way through. And I feel more real when I'm with you."

Then virtual Flynn reached out and squeezed her hand. "Alright. Thanks. I'll meet you tomorrow on Level 25 at the intersection of P and Q." Then with a racing heart, he disconnected from the call before he said anything to spoil it.

Back in his own living unit, Flynn touched the cloud access port in his ear and ended his holo call. He checked his wristband to see how long he had been in session; it read, "Holo call. Deirdre Callaghan. 7 minutes." Then he looked up from the couch to find his mother staring at him intently.

Clare said, "Finally, you're back. We have to talk about this again."

Flynn made a dramatic exhale and heaved himself up off the couch. He took one glance at his mother and stalked off to the bathroom. "Talk away, but I'm not listening."

Clare Brennan followed close behind him, taking small quick steps and wringing her hands. She said, "When your cloak fell at the ritual, I saw the Medical Director looking at you. You were seen, Flynn. We can't go on like this. It's too dangerous for you."

Flynn made it to the bathroom first and closed the door in her face. Clare placed one hand on the door and leaned her face into the crack to speak. Her voice trembled and she said, "Son, I just think that maybe it's time to tell the truth. The Medical Director saw your condition today."

From within the bathroom he said, "It was an accident, alright? I didn't plan to be seen."

Clare begged, "We need to go to him and plead for mercy about what we kept hidden. If we don't go to them now, it will be too late. Maybe he will help you. The last one wanted to help you, remember?"

In the small bathroom, Flynn planted both elbows on the sink and rested his head in his hands, his tense fingers knotting themselves in his short hair. He spoke again to his mother, biting off each word to keep himself from yelling at her. "Oh, the Ministry provides, is that what you believe? I know he saw me. And I saw him too. The way he studied me. If I reveal myself to that Medical Director it will be nothing but experiments."

Clare said, "The Ministry will forgive us for what we have kept hidden if we go to them willingly. I'm sure of it."

"Let me tell you what going to them will be like for me: 'Take this pill, but watch out for side effects including eyeballs falling out of your head, tooth itching, growing an extra toe, and spontaneous combustion.' And that's if things go well for me. You know...if they LIKE me and all."

In a pleading tone she said, "They could stop this disease, or maybe even reverse it. Don't you want to be like everyone else?"

"For Makers' sake," Flynn yelled. "Volunteering myself will do nothing to change their reaction. I don't trust them. And I don't understand why you do. This is how I am. Just let me be."

Clare started to cry and speaking again was difficult. "But sweetheart, what if they can make you better? It's been years since you were evaluated. Maybe they can offer you something. We have to try."

"Ma, you know what Dr. O'Boyle said when I was young. 'The Ministry will never tolerate someone like you. The ruined are hated and you will be treated as one of them. Banishment.' Is that what you want for me? Why do I have to be the one to remind you?"

Flynn's patience was worn through. He looked at his face in the mirror, noticing the fine lines around his jaw and the stubble of a full beard that marked him no matter how often he shaved. Whenever he saw himself, he saw what everyone in Skellig City feared most of all – getting old. He rubbed his aching knee. Last week, his shoulders had started to hurt too. None of it was fair. In a whisper to himself he said, "Why are you spending time with me, Dee? I'm sick. And hideous by most everyone's standards. And you. You're so beautiful and smart and brave. Just about perfect in every way. You could have any boy you want after Selection. Maybe you just feel sorry for me after all."

He clenched his left fist and punched the looking glass over the sink. The mirror cracked, and blood began to well up across his knuckles where the shards had cut in. He yelled, "No more doctors for the rest of my life, Ma. It's my secret, and I'm going to keep it."

Clare said, "But I want to try. For you."

Exasperated, Flynn put his hands over his eyes. Some blood got on his face. In a quiet voice that was more alarming than any yelling would have been, he stated, "Ma, is it that I need to try or that you need me to? I'm always going to be a freak. I'm always going to have to hide. Maybe you should start accepting it."

With that, Clare cried the harder. Flynn could tolerate hiding and the fear of getting caught. But for him, the worst thing of all was pity. He was truly unprotected from pity. So he opened the bathroom door and brushed his mother aside.

Clare exclaimed, "Flynn! You're bleeding."

He ignored her and went immediately to his bedroom and locked it. "Leave me alone." He wiped the blood off on his pants leg and pressed hard on the cuts to stop the bleeding. Then with no one looking, he sank to the hard tile floor and rested his head against his knees. To himself he whispered, "What do you see when you look at me, Dee? If a girl like you could love me...I would feel...I would feel like I could do anything. Blast it. We have to get out of here before they find me."

Sighing, he got up and climbed into bed. He checked his wristband to see how many dream credits his mother had transferred to his profile. He had a few to spare until their argument died down and he could ask for more. Then reaching for his earbud again, he accessed the cloud. He fell asleep instantly as the data transmission was conveyed wirelessly to his mind. Credits were deleted from his profile by the Dream Administration system and his wristband logged the change.

Dream 156892, *White Noise*, was one of the handful of dreams he could afford on his mother's small salary. It was just a set of sounds; no pictures or Matchers were in it. It was composed of the everyday noises of the city; people rushing to and fro, children complaining, and the sound of the lifts opening and closing. For the dreamer, it was like walking invisibly among the city dwellers. The dream was one of his favorites: it was cheap, and it provided a place where he didn't have to hide.

And so sleeping Flynn listened to their voices and watched their daily life. He even wondered if some of them might be ageing, like him. Different.

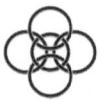

Back in the Callaghan living unit, Deirdre was downloading her mother's dream at the same moment. She rolled over on her creaky mattress, pulled up the covers, and touched her cloud access earbud. In less than a second, she was asleep and entered *Red Oak*, Dream 482036.

Deirdre stepped into what first seemed like a place on fire. Everything was glowing red and golden yellow. She gasped then brought her arm up across her eyes to shield herself from the blaze. But she felt no heat. So she peered out from behind her arm and saw no flames, only colored leaves dancing on the breeze. Sunlight streamed from the sky, coating each leaf as it turned this way and that on the subtle air currents. She brought her arm down and found herself surrounded by a forest of trees in full autumn bloom. There were hundreds of oaks in every direction she looked, their wide gnarled trunks ending in an explosion of color at the top.

She looked around and waited for the dream to unfold but nothing happened, so she watched the leaves float on the breeze and waited. Then a piece of opaque parchment drifted toward her, mixed in with the red leaves. It floated and twisted on the wind until finally the breeze brought it to Deirdre's feet. She reached down and picked it up. It was written in a scrawling gold script that she had never seen before. The words read, "What is your favorite color, Dee?"

The color purple flashed in her mind. Looking down, she found herself clothed in a full-length dress, with leather and wood sandals on her feet. Gone were the Skellig City greys. The fabric was a deep violet, embroidered around the neckline and upper arms with a delicate silver thread. The dress felt like it had been made just for her. She brushed her hands across the fabric and the butterfly sleeves fell almost to her knees, even when her arms were outstretched. She could tell at once that this was a special dream, not the usual empty plots of the ones the Ministry made and sold. She felt aware in it, like she could control things more than she ever had before.

Then another piece of parchment drifted toward her. She reached up and grabbed it off the breeze. This one said, "Go anywhere you desire. This world is yours." The trees started to sway and great oaks bent aside. A tamped earth path opened up through the forest and wound through them. Sunlight hit the path in pools of light and a few fresh red leaves drifted into the light. Deirdre couldn't see where the path went, but she felt happy just looking at it.

Being careful with her beautiful garments and unfamiliar footwear, she started along the path. She could feel the texture of the cloth on her skin and the light touch of falling, moist leaves on her face and neck. She knew that the dream was her mother's because the visuals were so beautiful. But Deirdre could also feel Maeve's presence in the delicate sensations of clothing and leaves on her skin. Now she knew why her mother wanted her to preview this dream after everything that had happened in the Ritual Room. Even with Maeve gone, she could see the whole of her mother's gift – the ability to find Maeve through dream whenever she wanted.

Further down the path, she heard the clash of wood against wood. Following the sound, she came to a break in the trees where crumbling stone ruins marked a long-abandoned residence. The structure was open on two sides where the stones had fallen away, and ivy curled through the stones that remained. The entrance wall was intact and through a stone archway she saw two warriors in short capes (one black, one grey) dueling back and forth across the plank flooring. The man in black looked like part of the forest with his flaming red hair. They swung their wooden staffs with precision and ferocity, each trying to land a strike on the other's body.

A slight woman in a cream and gold full-length gown kneeled in the entrance facing Deirdre and the forest. She had her back to the warriors behind her, and she seemed to give no thought to the fight or her own safety. She looked stoically out into the forest, her hair pulled into a ponytail behind her. She looked right through Deirdre, as if she wasn't there.

Entranced, Deirdre stepped closer. Each attack rang out with the crack of wood connecting. The fighters moved back and forth across the platform, exchanging blows with deadly speed. They were evenly matched, and every new attack was deflected by the other. Deirdre wanted to run forward and stop the fight, but she hesitated, not sure how she could.

With contempt in his voice, the warrior wearing grey called out, "I could run you through without even flinching."

Again their two staffs clashed together. The warrior in grey pushed against the warrior in black, repelling him a few steps backwards. Then the black warrior slipped on the leaves that had collected on the plank floor. The grey warrior pressed his advantage, pulled out a knife, and sliced into the arm of the other. His blood flowed freely. Stumbling back and trying to regain balance, the black-robed man returned a blow. Though misaimed, it was enough to force his opponent back and foil the glint of the knife.

Again their two staffs rang out with the piercing snap of wood on wood. The black warrior was losing more and more blood. The leaves swirling across the floor of the amphitheater were now coated in the slick red of his life force, red on red. Then abruptly, the fighter in black kneeled on the hardwood floor, laid down his staff, and offered his chest to the other man. He flung his arms wide and said, "Grey warrior! Perhaps you could run me through without flinching, without a thought for the life of another. And I now say, do it. Slice me in half. I won't flinch, for I am prepared for the Otherworld. If you can say the same, then take my life." The words of the black warrior were like an electric shock for young Deirdre. She felt something stirring inside herself, like one petal of a long dormant flower bud that was finally free to open.

A new and even deadlier battle of wills now raged in the stone ruins. The grey warrior was poised with his knife in the air, ready to take the last slice that would end the black-robed man's life. The black warrior kneeled on the floor with his chest bared. Both men held themselves there, motionless. Each man considered who was stronger, the physical warrior or the spiritual one. Just at the breaking point, the grey warrior lowered his knife and fell to one knee before the man in the black cloak.

The grey warrior said, "You are the higher master. I yield." Then he took his staff and broke it across his knee. He laid it before the other man and walked off into the forest.

Suddenly, the scene shifted. Deirdre looked down and found herself kneeling on the wooden floor of the amphitheater covered in the cream and gold dress. She murmured, "Now I am her."

She rose to her feet as the black warrior walked toward her. The knife from the battle was in one hand and he placed it in hers. Deirdre felt the cold metal against her skin. The warrior curled her fingers up around the blade, drawing tiny droplets of blood as the knife bit into flesh. He said, "It belongs to you now, lady. As do I. My name is Roenin. And I shall prepare you for what is to come."

The last thing Deirdre remembered was the swirling sensation of autumn leaves on the back of her neck.

Deep inside Skellig Michael, the citizens of the city slept with wild abandon. Each minute spent in dream was release from a life lived in the dark and under concrete. The dreamers in the city could all be found in their cots, some with peaceful smiles on their lips, while others' fingers twitched with excitement. As long as you followed the rules, earned your credits, and spent them on dreams produced by the Makers, you could find your escape in the night. But without the dreams there was no sleep and each dream download came at a price. If you didn't work, your credits ran out quickly.

With their dreams, the people pretended that the Dream Drones' boot steps and the 'Mare punishments weren't happening. And they tried not to think about what would happen if the dream credits ran out. They could be young forever in fantasies supplied by the Makers. Because the dreams created by them were so real, so enticing, everyone labored so that they could buy more. Whatever sensory pleasure you wanted, you could find it in dream. The people were grateful for the scratchy clothes and meager Nutripaks, as long as the dreams kept pouring forth from the Makers. The phrase "The Ministry provides," passed across their lips as easily as breath or food. They were dependent. Hooked.

The marketing masters of the Dream Administration sold each dream on the holo screens as the answer to whatever ailed you. "Feeling lonely? Find new romance in Dream 203486. Is the age of descent approaching? Be young again as Maura, our Dream Match winner from 3075. Want a little luxury from head to toe? Win a spa package in Dream 821677." So the people kept working and buying and working and buying. But the more that they dreamt, the emptier they felt. And the more they dreamt, the harder it was to rest without a download.

Late that same night while the rest of the city was in dream, one man sat awake in his office. He tapped his finger on the table and looked at a yellowing medical illustration hanging on the wall. The framed picture showed the human brain and where the neurotendrils of the weaver grew into it. He felt a feeling of pride looking at it.

Medical Director Odran Shea was perched over his desk, a bird-like quality to his face. The work table was standard-issue for the Minister's top administrators, and projected a hologram of file icons onto the surface of the table. Odran reached out to the file labeled *Flynn Brennan Medical File* and tapped it twice to open it. Out of the icon spewed pages of documents, and they arranged themselves in a grid-like pattern across the display.

Odran tapped on each document in sequence, enlarging it so the type could be read. But page after page was empty except for a stamp that gave a date and read, 'Deleted.' Odran's fist tightened and he whispered, "Gone. Every medical note on Flynn Brennan has been erased." He sat back in his chair and closed his eyes. He sat that way for some time, his mind searching for a way around the barrier of the missing records.

"Hmm," he said. "How to find what has been hidden?" Then he spoke to the cloud's voice interface. "Computer. Cross-reference the date-of-service stamps in the Flynn Brennan file against dates of all lab tests ordered. Execute." Odran steepled his fingers and put his elbows on the desk while he waited for a response.

A brassy female voice filled the room. It said, "Findings returned. On the days Flynn Brennan was seen in clinic, 57 tests were ordered by the prior Medical Director."

Odran said, "Cross-reference those 57 tests with keywords *genetic defect, biological markers, aging*. Execute."

The female voice came on again. "One match. Name of test: Aging Genetic Marker Panel."

"And the results of the test?" Odran asked.

"Deleted."

"Got ya," he whispered, a tight smile curling across his teeth.

3

Voice 1: "Look, people. We need a slogan, and it needs to be good. I'm not going up there with what we have so far."

Voice 2: "Well, what are we pitching the customer? Dreams, fantasies, what?"

Voice 3: "How about *Book a week at Skellig City Resort. Live an entire lifetime in one night*?"

Voice 4: "*Dream with IDream - a different fantasy every night.*"

Voice 5: "No, no. I've got it. *Be young again, with IDream.*"

Voice 2: "That's it, team. Buy back what you lost. *Be young again with IDream.*"

Voice 1: "We're going to make a killing."

- Meeting Transcript, Marketing Team, Dream cloud archive
March 1, 2043

The next morning, Deirdre woke up to the sound of her usual wake-up call through her earbud device. She groaned inwardly; she didn't want to leave the world of *Red Oak*. As she lay in bed, she tried to remember the events in the dream: the staff fight, the fire-red trees, and how Roenin had won his battle by offering himself up. *Roenin. Who are you really? Why were you so important to Maeve?* Deirdre listened to Breck's breathing from

45

the bunk below her and closed her eyes again. She brought back the feeling of the dream and imagined her bedroom swirling with whirlpools of red leaves. Opening her eyes again to the drab grey walls and stark furniture was a disappointment. *Blast. Why can't our classes start late like Breck's?*

Deirdre made her way out of bed, dressed in grey tunic and pants, grabbed her day sack, and headed to the kitchen for a Nutripak. *Will it be A, B, C, or D today?* She grabbed Flavor A of the Type II food and headed out the door for school without waking anyone. Deirdre sucked down the remainder of breakfast and stepped into the lift to Level 25. Still distracted by thoughts of *Red Oak*, she absentmindedly wound through the hallways to section P. At the four-way intersection, she saw Antrim, smiling and waving to her.

"Morning, cutie," said Deirdre.

"Hey you," replied Antrim, tucking a red wave of hair behind her ears. Antrim was standing with her back against the wall, her day sack at her feet. Deirdre joined her and placed her own sack on the floor next to Antrim's.

To pass the time while they waited for Flynn, Deirdre asked, "What did you dream last night?"

Antrim replied, "Dream 223719, *Lazy Beach*. It's pretty simple; you just laze around on a beach blanket in the tropics. Some pretty island, whatever. Totally boring, so you wake up ready for something interesting."

Antrim made Deirdre smile. Tiny, with a high-pitched, lilting voice and small stature, Antrim could charm anyone.

Deirdre said, "Sounds relaxing. And dull."

Antrim asked, "How about you? What did you dream?"

Deirdre replied, "A new dream that my Ma is working on. Antrim, it was amazing. I opened my eyes and first I thought that the place was on fire. But it wasn't. It was filled with trees, as far as I could see. And the leaves were like red films, shaped like your hand but thin, so you could see the light through them. That was what made it look like fire, because the light from the sky showed through all of them. And lots of them were coming away from the branches and drifting through the air, almost like it was their time or something. But how would a plant know to do that? Can you imagine it? My Ma really worked hard on this one. It's not like any of the other dreams I've been in."

Antrim's eyes were wide. "That sounds incredible! I wonder if my uncle will spring for it when it's released to the catalog." Then Antrim reached out and put a hand on Deirdre's shoulder. "Oh glitch, Dee. I forgot to ask you about Maeve. Are you ok?"

Dee's eyes got a little red. "I was feeling pretty low afterwards, thinking about her standing in the cylinder. Afraid. Antrim, what do you think is really waiting for us at the bottom of that thing?"

Antrim hesitated and looked up the hall and back again. "Gosh, Dee. I don't want to even think about it or I get all creeped out. I just tell myself it's the way to Tír na nÓg and try to think of something else."

Deirdre said, "Yeah. I know what you mean. And that dream I told you about? Well, Maeve worked on it with my mother. So I felt like maybe she's not totally gone."

Antrim leaned in and whispered, "That's good, Dee. But have you talked to Flynn since yesterday? Are you sure he should be going to school today? After...you know...at the ritual?"

Deirdre said, "I did holo him last night before dream. I told him he has to be more careful. He doesn't seem too worried about it though. But that's Flynn. Pinch him and he smiles, just so you know you didn't get to him. Anyway, what's taking him so long this morning?"

Flynn rounded the corner just then. "Morning, beauties," he called out in his flirtatious but harmless manner. Deirdre felt her face get a little flushed at the sight of him, but then the color drained right out of it.

Even though he was a full section length away, Flynn could see her face clearly. He faltered as her face read, "Be careful. They're here." So he wrapped his cloak more tightly around himself and kept walking.

Looking up the hallway beyond Flynn, Deirdre had spotted two red-uniformed Dream Drones rounding the corner behind him. Antrim saw them too and she pulled in close to Deirdre, half hiding behind her. Drones always patrolled in pairs, their black boots clicking in unison with every step. Flynn brought the cloak up across his face and continued walking. They were right behind him. He was exposed. He could be noticed.

Deirdre forced her eyes to the floor to avoid eye contact with the Drones. She slyly watched their boots approach from under lowered eyelashes. *Why does it feel like something else is staring out from behind all that red? Nice and easy, Flynn. Just keep walking.* Deirdre felt out for some hint of humanity, but there was nothing. Flynn kept his pace, walking steadily about ten feet in front of the soldiers.

Both were female Drones in their twenties with blank stares plastered on their faces. Fortunately, their eyes were their natural colors: blue for one woman and green for the other. This meant that they were not in Dream Justice mode...yet. There was no good kind of Drone, but the kind you could work around was in semi-Dream. Red in the eyes meant that you had been noticed, and being noticed was always bad. The Ministry saw through their eyes, felt with their hands, and executed Dream Justice through them as it saw fit.

Flynn reached Deirdre and Antrim and came to a stop against the wall with them. Everyone kept silent. The Drones marched past, faces forward, and crossed through the four-way intersection. Three pairs of eyes followed them down the hallway. Still, no one said anything.

But then something went wrong. The Drones turned back toward them, red light flashing up the passageway from their eyes. Their scanning routines had flagged something. Deirdre shot an arm out, pressing Antrim and Flynn back against the wall. *Not Flynn. Please, not Flynn.*

Just then, a man ran into the intersection from the other hallway and stopped, frozen in the corridor. His clothes were ripped, and he was out of breath. For a second, no one in the hallway moved. Then, everyone exploded. The Drones broke into a run, shouting for the man to stop. He started running too, up the way Flynn had come. Deirdre could hear his panicked breath.

The three friends watched one Drone load a 'Mare onto her wristband device. Antrim grabbed onto Deirdre's arm and squeezed it tightly. The Drone fired and the data transmission snaked up the hall toward the runner. But he was ready for it, and dove onto the floor as soon as he heard the snap of the 'Mare firing. It missed him, but the Drones kept coming.

The man scrambled to his feet and ran a few more steps to a locked door on the hallway. Despite his panic, it looked like he knew where he was going. The man banged his fists on the door. They were still in the residence levels so Deirdre knew it must be someone's home. He shouted, "Come on, man. You have to let me in!"

The Drones were almost on him. Then the door opened and another man stepped out and shoved the runner away from his door. His long blond hair was tied in a ponytail and it whipped around his neck. He said, "Lad, I don't know you. Get on your way." The runner fell back, stumbling into the approaching Drones. His arms flailed and he looked sick when the closest Drone grabbed onto him. The blond man just stood in his doorway and stared.

The other Drone prepared another 'Mare burst. The runner struggled and kicked, but the woman in the red uniform held him tight. In a flat voice she said, "You are arrested for attempting to access the cloud as a Maker. Impersonating a Dream Maker is a serious offense. Is there anything you wish to say about this other man, Cashel Quinn, to reduce your sentence?"

Deirdre took a step forward, but Flynn pushed her back again. He whispered, "No, Dee. You will only make it worse for him."

The runner stopped struggling; he knew he was caught. "No. I was just looking for a door. Any door."

The other woman leaned toward him and said, "Any door, you say? Cashel Quinn, step aside. Your living unit will be searched." Cashel stepped away from the entrance and the Drone strode forward. Glancing back at the runner, she said, "The Ministry will make its own assessment." Then she disappeared through the doorway, leaving everyone in the hallway.

No one spoke. None of them dared to even glance at one another. From inside Cashel's space came the sounds of furniture being overturned, cupboards being emptied, and toiletries being strewn about. The minutes dripped by. Then the Drone came back out and addressed Cashel. "No contraband was found within your living quarters, Cashel Quinn. However, your name is now on the

Ministry's watch list. Twenty dream credits will be deducted from your profile on the suspicion of aiding this impersonator. I advise you not to have another infraction. Good day."

Cashel continued to stare at the floor and replied, "The Ministry provides."

The Drone turned back to the runner and said, "Your sentence is two months lived experience of 'Mare. Your body will be stored in Dream Justice while you live out your dreamlock. Your normal work duties will then commence with a reduced rate of pay. Under surveillance, of course." The man cringed and whimpered, but the Drone didn't notice. She raised her device and fired again.

This time, the pulse hit its mark and the man slumped over, unconscious. His eyes darted back and forth under closed lids and he went immediately into REM. The Drones dragged the man's body away, and Cashel remained in the doorway a moment longer. He looked at the three friends up the hall with eyes that said, "Get out of here, kids." Then he went back into his unit and shut the door.

When the Drones were gone, Flynn looked at the two girls and whispered, "Underground for sure."

Antrim grabbed Deirdre's hand. She looked into her friend's eyes and struggled to find words. One thing terrified Antrim through and through: being selected for Dream Drone duty when she turned 16. She said, "Dee, what do you think it would be like to be converted into a Dream Drone? How do they even do it?"

Deirdre said, "I only know a few things from overhearing Ma and Da. Once Selection is made, they are hidden somewhere in the city. They go through some kind of conditioning, so the Ministry can control them better. The arachnoid they get is different, somehow. But Antrim, neither of us is going to fail in Selection, and neither of us is going to find out."

Antrim dropped Deirdre's hand and stared after the Drones, even though they had turned the corner and were gone. "But how can you be sure? You remember what happened to Liam last year. He was a smart, funny, good-natured guy. What made them select him? I see him in the hallways now and then, dressed in his red uniform and black boots. But he's just gone. It's horrible."

Anger welled up inside of Deirdre and she grabbed her friend by the shoulders. "Antrim, c'mere. I'm not going to let them take you. No matter what happens at our Selection. We're going to be right in the recovery room, waiting for you. Flynn and I... well. Just trust me, ok?"

"Ok, Dee. Ok." Antrim smiled slightly, but it barely turned up her cheeks.

Together the three gathered their things and made their way on to school. When they passed by Cashel's doorway on their way to the lift, Deirdre fell back from the other two and took a long look at the man's door. *I wonder if he really is underground?*

Flynn turned back to Deirdre and called, "Coming, slayer?"

"Sure. Sure I am."

The three friends stepped off the lift, each a little rattled by the events with the runner. The school section took up the entire 12th level. The Ministry wanted its populace well-trained to serve its interests, and so every square foot had been devoted to preparing the young for their lines of service. The entrance was guarded by two more Dream Drones and a set of identity scanners. Deirdre hated the coldness of the machines, and the daily task of passing through them. *Why does school need security? To make sure no one steals their mandatory free lessons?* Deirdre, Flynn, and Antrim stepped through one by one as the scanners connected to their cloud access earbuds and confirmed their identity profiles.

A metallic voice rang out, "Deirdre Callaghan, identify confirmed. Flynn Brennan, identity confirmed. Antrim O'Connor, identity confirmed."

Then they were through and carried along by the current of young people all scurrying to their classes. Like all of the hallways in Skellig City, the walkways in the school were lined with holo screens advertising the latest and greatest dreams for sale. The screens activated automatically, triggered wirelessly by the age profile for whoever passed by. The Ministry promoted their dreams everywhere and all the time.

As the three walked through the hall, one of the holo screens switched on. A voice boomed and flickering pictures formed. "Now offering *Casino Legacy* for the special price of 1800 credits," the voice said. An image of a luminous casino floor filled the screen, with gamblers waving at the rushing teens. "While away those nighttime hours as a wealthy heiress or champion of business! Gamble in high-stakes games and get the girl! Or guy! This download features last years' Dream Match winners, Sinead and Aiden. Don't forget, Dream 745937."

Deirdre, Flynn, and Antrim ignored the ad and just kept walking. Other kids paused in the hallway, sending ticker messages to their parents with the catalog code for the dream and a message to buy it.

Further down the hallway they were hit with another advertisement, triggered by some of the younger children rushing by. "Kids, make your parents buy this one for you! Dream 702737, *Lazy Frog*, lets you become the ruler of the lily pad pond as you laze the day away. Other frogs have to bring you treats and do tricks for you. All the other kids are dreaming this one for 500 credits!"

"Get them while they're young," Deirdre mumbled.

A pair of boys next to the holo screen put their noses up to the hologram. One reached in to stick his finger in the pond and said, "Look, it's *Lazy Frog*! I wish Ma would get that one for me."

The second child replied, "I've got it. It's cool. But I like *Race Car Runner* better. It's Dream 3729..." Their voices faded into the distance as Deirdre, Flynn, and Antrim entered the locker area.

Antrim put her midday Nutripak into her locker and slammed it shut. She turned to Deirdre and asked, "What class do you have first?"

Deirdre said, "It's the middle of the week, so Flynn and I have Kinesthetic Communication. But we'll see you for Visual Technology Interface for third period. Try not to worry today, k?"

"K, but just 'cause you're the one asking," smiled Antrim sweetly. Then she turned and made her way through swarming students to get to class.

Flynn and Deirdre headed off in the opposite direction. But before they reached first period, Flynn pulled Deirdre aside and said, "Can we hold off on going to class for a sec? I want to talk about Blue Sky. Outside the holo room."

Deirdre replied, "Sure." She moved closer to him so they could speak in a whisper without being heard by the other students.

Flynn looked in her hazel eyes and whispered, "Dee. What if we do get out of here? What do you want for yourself? On the surface."

She said, "It's operation Blue Sky, isn't it? I want to find it. See it with my own eyes and not through some data packets transmitted through the Ministry. And Maeve told me about grass. I want to see that too and feel it between my toes. It's green. Did you know?"

Flynn smiled. He felt good about being so near to her. Feeling her breath against him was exhilarating. "You do have cute toes," he said.

Deirdre blushed a little and said, "What about you, Flynn? What do you want when we get out there?"

Flynn reached out and brushed a strand of hair away from her face. For a moment, he looked tenderly into her eyes. Then he looked down and took a deep breath. In halting words he said. "What do I want? What I want is..."

But then a group of Matchers passed by on their way to class and one of the boys deliberately bumped into Flynn, their shoulders hitting hard against each other. In an instant Flynn's eyes shifted from sky blue to the dark, hard blue of a thunderstorm. The Matchers moved on and laughed.

Deirdre pulled back a little; Flynn could be unpredictable when his eyes turned like that. And she wanted sky blue Flynn back. So she reached out to him with a soothing voice and said, "Come on. Let's get to class. They don't matter, remember?"

It didn't always work, but this time it did. The clouds drew back and Flynn smiled again. "You're right. Come on then." The two of them headed to class.

Deirdre moaned inwardly as she and Flynn entered the brightly lit classroom. *First period is always dead. Probably duller than Lazy Beach.* She saw Mr. MacAleese at the front of the room sitting at his desk and elbowed Flynn. "Maybe you will get selected for the Education Division."

Flynn whispered back, "And what would I teach? How to be snarky?" They shot each other knowing smiles as they walked past the instructor.

The front row of the class was filled with Matchers, Deirdre's least favorite classmates. Dressed in their colorful outfits and puffed-up hair, they were hard to miss. The Ministry went to great lengths to groom its future stars of the dream world, providing them with wardrobe, make-up art, and any surgical manipulation that would bring them to physical perfection. They embodied beauty for its own end, a closed loop that never went anywhere in Deirdre's opinion. But everyone else saw them differently. Matchers began building a platform early with their elaborate costumes, selling their brand to any who would look or listen. A Dream Match winner's job was to seduce the entire city, and they wooed everyone obsessively. They wanted stardom and the luxury that went with it, no matter the personal costs.

Walking to her seat, Deirdre passed through the group of Matcher girls. All five were clothed in all the manufactured beauty that the Ministry could muster. They were like wax dolls with their perfect features and glittering outfits. As Deirdre brushed by, the girls on either side of the walkway bent to whispering. The one on the left was named Fianna, and her outfit made Deirdre wonder if there had been an explosion in the dye room. Blue, purple, yellow, and orange covered her from head to toe. She even had feathers sewn into the collar of her tunic, making her look like some exotic stuffed bird. The other girl was named Shauna. Covered in metallic shades of gold, silver, and bronze, it was hard to separate her sparkling face from her glittered clothing.

Fianna whispered. "Grey just doesn't do anything for anybody. I'm so glad we don't have to wear it."

Shauna whispered back, "I know. Wouldn't that be the worst part about losing the competition? Having to wear those awful outfits?" Deirdre set her eyes forward and kept walking. The biggest insult you could pay to one of the Matchers was to ignore them.

But when Flynn walked by, Shauna spoke loud enough to be heard. "And there's Flynn. Patchwork cloaks are the hottest accessory this year." She then glanced at Fianna to see her reaction. Snickering some more, Shauna pulled a nail file from a sequined bag that hung at her side and began filing away.

This wasn't the first time that the Matchers had teased Flynn about his cloak. He had stitched the hood on himself and so it did look a little rough around the edges. Like Deirdre, Flynn kept his eyes up and away from them, so he didn't notice when Shauna stuck her foot out to trip him.

Deirdre whirled around to find Flynn sprawled on the floor. By this point, most of the class was laughing, especially the other Matchers. Shauna and Fianna gave each other high fives as Deirdre helped Flynn up. "Stop it," Deirdre shouted. Don't you care about anything but yourselves? Come on, Flynn. Don't pay any mind to them. They're as thick as manure but only half as useful." She gave him a hand and helped him up.

"Sure, Dee. You're right," Flynn said. He was boiling inside, but he wanted to get out of the center of attention as soon as possible. So he pulled the cloak close around his head and started walking. They made it to their seats at the back of the class just as Mr. MacAleese called everyone to order.

The teacher's main feature was his huge red nose which he always rubbed with the back of his hand. "Now class, settle down," he said. "And I'm especially talking to you Matchers. Today we are beginning unit six of Kinesthetic Communication. I want everyone to tap into the cloud using your earbud access ports. By now you should have mastered the basic steps of using slight body movements to interface with the cloud. Remember, mouth the letters SCHOOL without speaking. You'll see the folder icon appear on the top of your desk. Then find Activity B in the

Kinesthetic Communication folder. You may also use your stylus as you please."

The quickest one in the class, Deirdre quickly had her letters submitted to the cloud. She found the Kinesthetic Communication folder and opened unit six with a tap on the holographic icon. Flynn had his activity up too, and winked at her when she turned his way. *At least he looks like he is feeling a little better.*

When Activity B finished loading, a glowing blue orb appeared in the air hovering before Deirdre's eyes. Its surface rippled like water, yet somehow it seemed like a solid that was lit from the inside. It was a hologram, projected through the cloud for her. More blue orbs of light blinked into the room as the other students loaded their exercises. Deirdre stared into her ball, admiring its surface and inner light. Hers was mostly blue but still caught tiny colorful reflections from the Matcher's costumes at the front of the class.

"Everyone ready?" Mr. MacAleese continued. "Now look at your glo ball. It's probably rotating on its own. The goal of this exercise is to gain greater control over the subtle hand and arm movements you will use to interface with the cloud. These foundational skills will be used in any work placement after Selection. As you already know, your 16th year Selection is coming up for all of you. I want everyone to position your hand in the air about waist high. You will notice that your ball follows your hand."

Deirdre did as instructed and wondered what would be chosen for her. *Selection. The dream that will determine the rest of their lives. And no one is going to even ask what we want to do.* She could be selected for any of the main service lines of the city. Dream Administration was one - the arm of the Ministry that managed the cloud and all dream transactions. There was also Dream Justice - the arm that implemented the Minister's rule of law. The most feared group in the city, they kept profiles on everyone. Then there were the sub-divisions that provided for food, shelter, clothing, and medical care. If she demonstrated a certain kind of aptitude, she knew that she could be enrolled at Dream Maker Academy, like her parents and Maeve.

Lastly there was the possibility of being chosen for Dream Drone - to give up her free will and serve at the pleasure of the state. Luckily, being part of a Maker family gave her an edge for the dream of Selection over most of the other students; novices to the Academy tended to be selected out of Maker families. And Deirdre would take even the Academy over Dream Drone. Pondering those options was depressing, and her glo ball drooped a little with her thoughts.

Most people slogged through their workday, counting the minutes on their internal timepieces until they could go home, suck down a Nutripak, and enter the dream world. But Deirdre didn't want to be like the rest of the city. She didn't care how many Matchers she could become in the dream world. *I want to feel more than the plain grey of Skellig City. I want to be bowled over by life. Somehow.*

The teacher cleared his throat and Deirdre realized that her daydreaming had been noticed. She quickly bent back to her glo ball and found that by using the slightest wiggle of her palm, she could keep her ball almost absolutely still, hovering like a tiny blue sun.

Mr. MacAleese got up from his chair and said, "I'm going to pair up a few of you to try something harder. Deirdre and Flynn will be together. Also, Iona with Daley, and Braden with Miren. Your task will be to toss your ball to your partner while catching the ball they toss to you."

Shauna raised her hand while Fianna sat in her chair and pouted. They were both having trouble with the exercise. Shauna said, "Mr. MacAleese. I'm going to win Dream Match. I don't understand why I have to learn this stupid stuff. It's not like I'm going to need it. Maybe the others do, but not me, surely."

The teacher cleared his throat. In a tone of sarcasm that was lost on Shauna, he said, "Well, Shauna. I always need advanced students who can be a model for the others. Now, can you do that for all of us?"

"Oh, all right," replied Shauna. "I'll be the silly model for the class. All eyes on me, everyone. How do you toss the ball?"

Mr. MacAleese gave the instructions. But Shauna's ball dropped onto the floor and just sat there. No amount of hand waving could get it going again. Deirdre and Flynn shared amused looks and went to work on their assignment, easily tossing their ball of light back and forth.

As the hour went by, the room was filled with a luminescence that brought an uncommon beauty to the halls of Skellig City. By the end of the class, most of the Matchers were still unable to catch a holo. Deirdre felt pleased about that, and then a little guilty. *Well, if they wanted my pity, they shouldn't have picked on Flynn.*

Then the door opened and the room fell silent. Deirdre's glo ball developed a small red blotch; in her world it was the color of fear. She whirled around and saw them at the front of the class: two red-dressed Drones and the Medical Director in his white lab coat. It was the moment Deirdre had feared ever since Flynn was exposed at Maeve's ritual.

Someone next to her whispered, "It's the Drones. I heard they're always half in dream, receiving orders wirelessly through the cloud."

Another said, "Yeah. But not those two. They're on full alert. See the eyes? All red."

Leading the pair of Drones, Odran spoke in a voice that hit the room with an icy frost. "Flynn Brennan. Please walk slowly to the front of the room. Do as you're told and there won't be any trouble for anyone else."

Flynn glanced sidelong at Deirdre and then stood up. A red flush came up into Deirdre's cheeks and she hissed, "No, Flynn! Don't go up there!"

But Flynn reached out from under his cloak and waved her off. His eyes met with Odran's and he started walking toward them. Deirdre jumped to her feet and climbed up on the seat of her chair. With one foot planted forward, she pointed at the Medical Director and shouted, "What has he done wrong? We deserve to know!"

If the class had felt a chill from the Medical Director a few moments ago, now they were feeling frostbite on their toes. Odran said, "I don't have to tell you anything, Miss Callaghan. But I will make a public safety announcement for all. Flynn Brennan is being put under medical quarantine for the welfare of the city." Then the two Drones marched forward and grabbed Flynn's arms, pinning them behind his back. Flynn struggled, but he had no chance against both Drones together.

Alarmed questions broke out from the Matchers at the front. One asked, "Is he sick?"

Another stood up from her desk and asked, "Can I catch it?"

Two other girls rushed to each other to inspect for symptoms, stretching eyes open and sticking out tongues. One exclaimed, "Do I look pale?"

The other said, "What if I've already got it?" They pinched each other's faces and looked terror-stricken.

Students all over the classroom jumped out of their seats, gestured wildly, and vied for the attention of the Medical Director. But one clear voice broke through the chaos. From her perch on her chair, Deirdre said, "There's nothing wrong with him. Everyone stop. He's fine." But the three men ignored her and started marching Flynn out of the room. The Director led and the Drones followed with Flynn thrashing in their grasp.

Deirdre hopped off her chair and ran straight after them into the hallway. *They can't do this.* She sped around the Drones and grabbed the white-sleeved arm of the Director. In a voice that carried more authority than her years she shouted, "You can't take him if there's nothing wrong with him."

One of the Drones turned its red gaze on Deirdre, registering her hold on the Director. He let go of Flynn, raised his arm, and struck her square across the collarbone. Deirdre was knocked away from Odran and fell to the floor, her head making a loud smack on the concrete.

"No!" shouted Flynn, and he went crazy on the Drone that was still holding him. He threw an elbow left and a kick right, but the Drone just clamped down on him harder. He twisted around with all of his strength, all the while bellowing, "Dee! Dee! Are you hurt?"

Flynn had almost writhed out of the soldier's grasp, but then the Drone who'd hit Deirdre turned back to Flynn and grabbed him by the back of the neck. With two on him again, he was locked down by four inhumanly strong arms. They lifted him up so they could look eyeball to eyeball. The Drone who'd hit Deirdre said, "Ok, lad. Now you've caught my attention."

With spite in his voice, the other Drone said, "Well, we have a situation here. Normally, I would sentence you both to a 'Mare. Attacking the Medical Director? Resisting quarantine? Flynn Brennan and Deirdre Callaghan, your violations will be recorded on your permanent Dream Justice profile."

Flynn yelled, "Just leave her alone!"

The Drone smirked and said, "But since you've been so pleasant to be around, Flynn, I'm going to offer you a once-in-a-lifetime deal. Either I sentence you both to Dream Justice, or Flynn, you get a double the fine and the Callaghan girl goes free. So, what's it going to be?"

A group of students were peering around the doorway of the classroom, trying to see without being noticed by the Drones. Deirdre rubbed her head and got up off the floor. But before she could say anything, the Drone grabbed her and pulled her over to where Flynn was being restrained.

Flynn said, "I'm the one that attacked you. So I'm the one that should be punished. Not her."

"No," cried Deirdre, looking at Flynn with pleading eyes.

But he wouldn't look back into hers. "You know what my choice is," Flynn said. "So get on with it. Dee, tell my mother where I am."

The Drone's smile widened. "Flynn Brennan, you are sentenced to 20 minutes of 'Mare 672084, six hours of lived dream experience. Be sure to enjoy yourself."

The Drone reached into his belt and pulled out a small device about an inch long. It got its name from a ravenous insect that swarmed upon any plant life, eating everything down to bare earth. It was used to send 'Mare content to anyone too young to have a weaver. Gasps went up from the other students watching them from the classroom.

One said, "The locust..."

Fianna raised her hand up to her mouth and whispered, "Not even Flynn deserves that."

The Drone held it tight in his fist while the other one set the chosen 'Mare to deliver. Flynn shook his head and tried to pull away but it was no use. Showing his crooked teeth through a half smile, the Drone flung the locust toward Flynn. Through the air it flew, its legs and wings expanding with every inch it came closer to its prey. It was a horrible sight, the ugly thing preparing to deliver its transmission. Everyone felt like it was happening in slow motion.

The locust landed on Flynn's forehead and its front legs pricked the skin above his eyes. They sunk into his flesh and the device began to do its work. The lights on the device burned a hotter red and Flynn's eyes rolled back into unconsciousness. The Drone dropped him and Flynn collapsed to the floor. The students looking on from the classroom drew back; no one wanted to watch.

The Drone let go of Deirdre too, and she fell to her knees beside Flynn. His face started to glisten with sweat and his eyes rolled frantically behind closed lids. The length of his 'Mare would feel like forever for him. She wanted to rip the locust off of his head, but she didn't know what that might do to him. Deirdre watched him with streaming eyes, her mind imagining a thousand different terrors Flynn might be living through. *All to protect me. One minute gone, nineteen left to go. This is all my fault.* She lowered her head to the cool hallway floor and grabbed Flynn's hand. *Stay with me. It will all be over soon. Can you tell I'm here? I'm right beside you. Flynn! Why didn't I tell you how I really feel about you?*

The Dream Drones busied themselves with filing their reports on the cloud. Then the Medical Director gave the next order. Motioning to one of the Drones he said, "You - escort Miss Callaghan to school detention. She will wait there until a parent comes to collect her." Then pointing at the other one he said, "You - pick up the boy. Follow me to the lockdown room in the medical unit. Also, prepare another dreamlock for him. I want him out until I decide how we will proceed."

The Drones did as instructed, pulling Deirdre and Flynn apart. Deirdre screamed and grabbed Flynn's cloak as she was hauled up and away. The other Drone threw Flynn's body over his shoulder, and then they were gone.

The Drone in charge of Deirdre kept her moving by following behind and poking her in the back. She staggered through the passageways of the school section, unable to think straight. *What are they going to do to him when he gets to the medical unit?*

Finally, they pushed through the double doors of the school administration area and Deirdre stumbled into the main desk. Like most things in the city, it was made of metal and she bumped her knees sharply on it.

The portly headmistress looked up from her access portal and gave Deirdre a sharp look. "I know I should be shocked whenever a student has to be escorted to my offices by a Dream Drone," she said. "But with your behavior, I stopped being surprised a long time ago, Deirdre Callaghan. And just so we're clear, that was not a compliment."

Deirdre replied, "Sorry, Mrs. Shanahan," as she fell into a plastic chair.

The Drone went to the desk to finalize Deirdre's transfer to the school authorities. The headmistress quickly connected to the cloud and brought up her holographic interface. From the reflections that moved across her face, Deirdre could see that she was scanning the report the Drones had filed.

"Attacking the Medical Director! With Flynn Brennan," she shrieked. "And a 'Mare sentencing of 20 minutes!" She turned to the Dream Drones. "That seems like a very severe punishment for a boy with no major priors."

The Drone that Flynn had kicked leaned toward the headmistress. Voice filled with suspicion, he asked, "Is there some complaint you would like to lodge with Dream Justice, Headmistress?"

Mrs. Shanahan tried to lick her mouth, but her lips stuck together like her saliva had just dried up. "No, Dream Drone. The Ministry provides. I will be sure to inform her parents of this violation when they arrive to collect her." Her eyes went back to the records in front of her.

The Drone pulled back and left the office. Deirdre forced herself to take a breath. Then she heard Mrs. Shanahan sending a ticker to her father, and her hands felt cold again. *As if getting Flynn sentenced to a 'Mare wasn't bad enough. Now Father is going to know all about it. I hate giving him something over me.* She sat quietly on the hard plastic chair and tried to calm her dread. *This is going to be worse than having a Drone after me.*

Deirdre sat on the chair while the minutes ticked by. Then Sean Callaghan swept into the room in his formal Maker robes. His face looked like it was frozen in stone. Without even glancing at Deirdre sitting against the wall, he walked right up to Mrs. Shanahan. "Hello, Headmistress. I received your ticker. Tell me what happened."

Sean listened closely as Mrs. Shanahan relayed all of the details of the last hour. Finishing her report, Mrs. Shanahan said, "Really, Dream Maker. We expect more from a daughter of yours."

Sean pressed his lips together in anger, making a thin flat line of them. As a Dream Maker, he wasn't used to being scolded; now Deirdre had two black marks against her. Silently motioning for Deirdre to follow, he left the office in long strides. Deirdre gave Mrs. Shanahan one long, unhappy look, then hurriedly caught up with him.

They rode the lift, then walked in silence all the way back to their living unit. Sean tucked his hands inside his orange robes and didn't say a word. Her father's stifling silence was almost worse to Deirdre than his yelling would have been. But she knew the yelling would follow once they arrived home. As soon as they crossed the doorstep, it began.

The door swung shut and he said, "How many times have I told you, Deirdre? You must obey the rules that the Ministry sets out for us. What were you thinking? Attacking the Medical Director? No. Don't answer that. Clearly you weren't thinking."

Deirdre turned her back on him and started to walk away. Sean called after, "You turn around this instant. We're done when I say we're done."

"I don't want to talk to you," she said.

"We are going to talk about it. Why would you risk everything this family stands for? And for what? Some boy who's been lying his entire life?" Sean put both hands on his head, as if to keep it from exploding.

Deirdre explained, "Da, I told the truth and things got out of hand. But..."

Sean cut her off, saying, "Is that what you think you did wrong? That you got caught? Haven't you heard anything that I've said over the last few years? You need to remain unnoticed. Why don't you understand that? Bad things happen when you stand out."

Deirdre said, "But Da..."

"Be quiet until I'm finished. What you did wrong was to disregard the regulations put forth by the Ministry. You know better, so I can only assume that you don't care. Is this how you treat your friends? You want them sentenced to Dream Justice because you can't keep your mouth shut?"

Her father had unintentionally struck Deirdre right where it hurt the most: her guilt that Flynn had taken the punishment for the both of them. The tension in the room was rising, and Deirdre lashed back at her father. "Actually, Da, I do care about my friends. But I know the real reason you're so upset. It's about your precious status as a Dream Maker. You're freaking out because the Callaghan name is now linked to a Dream Justice report. How will it be for you at the Academy knowing that everyone is talking behind your back?"

At this, Sean slammed both hands down on the main table and yelled with the full strength of his lungs. "You need to stay away from that boy! He is a risk you can't afford! He could jeopardize your chance of being selected for Maker. Go to your room, now. And don't come out until you've thought about what you've done!"

She turned away from him. Fighting back tears, Deirdre walked slowly to the room she shared with Breck and shut the door. Finally alone, she started to shake from all of the terrible things that had happened in the last few days. *I lost Maeve. Anything could happen to Flynn. And in a few days, I'm going to lose my mother too.* She stood there, with her back against the door, until her trembling died down. How long that took, she didn't even know. She was suddenly clear on one thing: that she didn't want to think or feel anymore. She had never used the dream world to escape her life before. But now, she climbed into her top bunk, accessed the cloud, and threw herself into the world of *Red Oak*.

I am walking down a path in the oak forest, watching leaves swirl around me on the crisp fall breeze. I am following the warrior in the black cloak. Suddenly, I am aware of his name again: Roenin. He is light on his feet and focused on some goal ahead. We must be going somewhere important. As twilight falls, the trees around me lose their red color and turn less beautiful, more ominous. We reach the end of the dense, silent forest and begin walking along a flagstone path leading to a massive castle.

The stonework is half shrouded in thick ivy, which rustles in the evening air. The path is lined with oil lanterns, glowing as if each one has a trapped firefly inside it. The castle we approach is even more ablaze with larger lanterns in red glass hurricanes. I am reminded of the red uniforms of the Dream Drones and shudder inwardly. Roenin looks over his battle dress at me.

"Ballycarbery Castle. We are close, lady. Be ready." We approach the massive front door of the fortress softly and silently. We both carry weapons, but I don't remember how the knife blade got into my hand. A servant stumbles into our path, carrying water on his way back from the well. Soundlessly, Roenin covers his mouth, snaps his neck with an iron grip, and lays his body silently on the grass. He motions me onward. The water from the servant's pail sloshes across the stone walkway. In this world, it seems natural to kill this way, hushed and quick.

Surprisingly, the front door to the castle is unguarded. We both press ourselves into the massive wood planks. The door is impressed with a knot pattern like our ritual jumpers. Hearing no voices inside, Roenin looks into my excited eyes, nods, and throws open the doors. They fly apart like leaves of paper being blown aside. We move into the main chamber, where a woman sits on a throne-like wooden chair - the same woman who had observed Roenin's duel earlier. She looks up at the sound of our entry, the surprise on her face quickly turning to anger.

"Sister," I say. Somehow, I know what I should do in this dream.

She throws me a hard, smoldering look, her face pinched and angular from too many years of jealous thoughts. She pulls two sticks from her long, black hair and lets her tresses tumble out across the folds of her dress. "I did not expect you back so soon, sister. In fact, I never expected you back at all. As you can see, I am reviewing the holdings of my new estate." Roenin unsheathes his sword and moves closer to our adversary.

I look at her and simply state, "The grey warrior is defeated, sister."

She retorts, "Oh please. The grey warrior is the finest fighter in the land. I advise you to be gone from here before he returns. Besides, I have calculations to conclude." She returns to her work, dismissing us.

I smile. "In fact, sister, he was defeated by his own code of honor. Perhaps the next champion you choose should not be so noble." I throw the two halves of his staff at her feet, a slight smile of victory on my face. The woman recognizes them immediately. Like an origami crane that is bigger on the inside, my sister's anger unfolds before me. How can someone so thin contain such rage?

"This isn't over," she spits.

"I'm sure it isn't," I sigh. "Now, it's time for you to go. Take your servants and never come back here." I sweep forward to take my rightful place in the seat of the house as my sister flies from the room.

Roenin looks upon me gravely. "You really should not have left her alive," he states with the matter-of-fact tone that only comes from years of taking life.

"Roenin, she's my sister. We share the same blood in our veins," I reply. Still, I wonder if he is correct.

He bows his head slightly and replies, "As you wish, lady. Your first battle is won. Come, let us tour the castle and make it yours again." He slides open the rich tapestry that separates the main room from the others, and I walk with him through the close stone hallways. My footsteps are softened by more tapestries on the stone floor. We pass empty room after empty room, each more magnificent than the last. The estate, my estate, is a marvel. There are sitting areas, music areas, and finally, what looks like a room for prayers.

I pause at the entrance to the sanctuary, which is shaped like a half circle off the side of the castle. The walls begin like the stonework of the rest of the estate, but gradually change and become the trunks of ash trees. Stone turns to living tree as my eyes follow the shape of the room. The apex of the room is all trees: what was made by man giving way to the life force of nature. The trunks become interlocking boughs near the top, forming the roof over my head. These leaves are the most beautiful green I've ever seen. This room sparkles for me, like a memory I just can't place.

I turn to Roenin and ask, "What is this place?"

He replies, "A place of worship, lady. All life was sacred to your ancestors. See the stonework turning to living tree? The sanctuary is here to show you that nature is the most powerful force in the universe and all things made by humankind must yield to it. The Ministry wants you to forget everything about your land. This room was built to be a guide for you."

I become excited. "You know of the land? What lies outside these walls?"

"Yes, lady. I know of it, from long, long ago. So many magical things were imagined by your people. Your ancestors, the druids, believed in the sacredness of all life and in another plane of existence beyond the physical one. All hidden from you now by the Ministry's Dream Protocol."

I wonder about this other plane. I look at my arm and tap on it. "You mean something other than this?"

"Yes, lady. A power inside every living thing sleeps and waits for anyone who will call to it. That power may have diminished, but here in the dream world, it can be *felt again and used for good. This is the only power that may shine light through the darkness of the Ministry."*

I ask, "When will this light come?"

He sighs and looks again toward the trees. "That, I do not know. But this room of sacred trees is a promise that it will be soon." He reaches forward and shows me the fresh green shoots on the branches. "I have waited long for the trees to stir. And now it has begun. But speak none of this outside of here; it is yet too dangerous. When the sanctuary trees are in bloom, then it will be time."

I study the lime-green shoots and feel suddenly joyful, like something inside me is beginning to grow as well. I step back to take in more of their beauty. Beneath the branches is an altar of sorts, the roots of the trees growing up to hold an object. I notice they form the five interlocking circles of the Dream Makers, and then I look closer at what the altar is holding. It looks like the teak box from our living unit, just missing our Callaghan family pattern on the top. What is that doing in this dream? I wonder why mother has placed our box here in the middle of the sanctuary.

I walked forward, reaching out to touch it like I have done a thousand times before at home. But Roenin's hand shoots out, stopping me from touching the wood. "No, lady. To touch it is death. You must promise me to never touch it, in here or out there."

I feel shock. "Wait. How do you know that this is the box in my home? Or about the Ministry's Dream Protocol?"

He is silent, and the dark pools of his eyes swallow me whole. Then he gathers up the cloth of his robe and in a twisting motion, swings it over my head. Everything goes dark and I feel myself falling backward into the trees. The fresh green shoots on the branches wrap around me and I remember nothing more.

The medical clinic where Flynn was held was blindingly colorless. Except for the red digital time display on the wall, everything was a sterile shade of white - the kind of white that makes a person feel constantly under attack. It was the next morning and Flynn came to slowly, shaking off the nightmare from the Drone's second 'Mare burst. When his blue eyes blinked open, he winced and put his hand across them. Gradually, he drew his fingers away, his eyes adjusting to the stark, uninterrupted brightness all around him. He groaned softly and rubbed his eyes with flat palms.

His situation was grim. He was laid out flat on a slab of something that felt like metal and made his muscles ache. He felt sluggish, like he had been drugged. Most insulting of all, his clothes had been taken and he found himself in his underthings. He didn't even want to think about who had undressed him.

Flynn forced his eyes all the way open and sat up, swinging his feet to the floor. He was in a small three-walled room about the size of a city bedroom. Beyond his holding area he could see a larger room dominated by a metal worktable at the center. It was littered with beakers, pipettes, and other things that looked more ominous: scalpels, syringes, and bottles of chemicals.

Seeing that there was no one there, he started for the worktable, his eyes fixed on one of the scalpels. But within a few steps, he ran into an invisible electrostatic barrier that separated him from the rest of the medical unit. "Blast it. Should've known there'd be a fourth wall," he said, rubbing his nose where he had bumped it.

His contact with the barrier tripped an alarm, and within moments the Medical Director breezed into the room. "Oh," he said, walking up to face Flynn on the other side of the barrier. "I see that your dreamlock has expired. Very good. Let us talk."

Flynn wrinkled his nose in a sniff and turned away. He sat back down on the bed and said, "That was a 'Mare? Haven't slept that well in years. I want my clothes."

Odran pulled up a stool and sat as well. "Your sense of humor is underwhelming. And you won't need your greys in here, lad. No visitors. Just you and I. And I don't care what you're wearing. Now, tell me about the doctor."

Keeping his voice even and light, Flynn asked, "What doctor?"

Odran snickered in a high-pitched tone that made him sound a little insane. Then he said, "You know the one. My predecessor, Neala O'Boyle. The doctor who deleted all of your medical records." The Director crossed his arms over his chest and adjusted his seat. He was a cat settling in until the mouse got tired.

"I don't see doctors," Flynn said. "And I don't want to start with you. Why am I in here? You know full well that I'm not contagious to anyone."

"Aren't you, lad? An idea is the most infectious thing there is. And you, Flynn, are an idea."

Flynn said, "I thought I was a lad. With lots of ideas. Now you say I am just one?"

Odran spoke faster now, "You infect people with tolerance. The ruined are not welcome here. They are hideous and you are one of them. Despite your birth record, we both know that you are one of them. And I have brought you here to prove it."

Flynn cocked his head and pushed back, needling the Director even more. "It does sound like you have something to prove. Are you sure it has to do with me?"

Odran put an edge in his voice. "You are a defect in the system. People must accept the cylinder at 35. This is our way, determined by the Ministry. The ruined must make space for the vital."

Flynn demanded, "And why must they?" He rose up off his metal bed once again.

Droplets of spittle forming on his lips, Odran said, "You see? You think your defect makes you special. That the rules the city lives by shouldn't apply to you. And if the whole city decided that the ritual didn't apply to them? That they could live until they fell apart and crippled the city with their needs? What then?"

Flynn was ready for him and pointed at the Director. "Then they could leave. Start their own city, and live as long as they want to."

The Director smiled again, regaining his composure. "There's only Tír na nÓg and the ritual, lad. Nothing else is out there."

Flynn asked challengingly, "How do you know there's nothing out there? What if there is something?"

"You've never been Topside, lad. If you had, you would know that there's nothing as far as the eye can see. Just a dead ocean and a barren coast."

Flynn's shoulders slumped as he heard those words. "I won't believe it. There's another way to live, if you would just let people choose for themselves."

Odran said, "This city and the Dream Protocol are all we have, Flynn. The Ministry provides, but it must also be protected. I'm not going to let you work against it."

"I don't want it protected. I want it torn apart."

"You are just as I thought you would be, Flynn. Different and dangerous. When I was a lad, I knew a boy like you. He wasn't happy with our rules. And he thought that people would listen to him if he kept at it, speaking out against our way of life. But I could see how dangerous he was. He was the sympathetic sort, and no one else was going to turn him in. So I had to take matters into my own hands. On the night before his Selection, I removed the marker from his door. And when the Drones came to collect him on his 16th birthday, they concluded that he had tried to evade the test. And do you know what happened next?"

"I assume you're going to tell me."

"He was taken for Selection anyway. And once his weaver was placed, he was sent for a 6-month dreamlock in cold sleep. And Flynn, it was then that I realized how I could best serve, no matter what my eventual Selection. I would do the dirty chores so that the Minister could keep his hands clean. I would assist him in ways he hadn't even dreamed of." Odran looked off into the distance and seemed to drift away to some fantasy playing in his mind.

Flynn's eyes turned almost black with anger. "You're crazy in the head."

Odran came back to himself and continued, "Ah, yes. Back to you, Flynn. I know exactly what you were seen for as a boy. A genetic panel will confirm your...abnormality. Your disease was not your fault, but how you have dealt with it is. Your lies and rule breaking are over. Once I verify your true biological age, you will be scheduled for an early descent. The ritual that all of the ruined must abide."

Flynn's face turned red as he ran at the barrier and pounded his fists against it. "What do you mean? I'm only 15!"

The Director stood up to leave. Over his shoulder he said, "The ruined must descend, Flynn. The city will be well rid of you." Then he was gone.

Flynn lay down on his bed once more. He was caught; it was over. There was only one thing he could think to do. He slowed his breathing so it would look to anyone watching like he was dozing. He felt certain that someone was. Then he rolled over and casually draped his hand across his mouth, hiding his jaw and lips. One thing was still in his favor: in the distraction that Deirdre had caused, they had forgotten to check for his earbud. It was still in place, and that meant he still had access to the holo rooms. From underneath his draped hand, he mouthed the letters that would place the call.

His body went limp and he opened his eyes in the holo room. There, he read the code off the ceiling of the room and sent a ticker message to Deirdre. It was early morning in the Callaghan unit. Deirdre was still in bed and hadn't yet left for school. She saw the message come through and then quickly placed her own call to the room where Flynn waited. Her image materialized wearing a grey nightgown.

Flynn stepped forward and gave her an awkward half-hug. Then he stepped back and said, "Dee. Did they hurt you? What happened after I went under?"

She said, "I'm fine. Just detention and an argument with Da. The usual. Are you alright? Where are you?"

"I'm in the med clinic. One of the quarantine rooms. Basically, I'm a prisoner. The Medical Director was here, Dee. It's bad."

Deirdre put her hand up to her lips. She said, "How bad? What are they doing to you?"

"Listen. They're watching me for sure. I can't be in this call for long. But Dee...they know."

She said, "How much?"

"He knows what to look for. Somehow he put it all together. And when he gets proof, I'm cooked."

Deirdre stepped forward and touched him on the arm. "How cooked?"

"An early descent, Dee. They know I'm ageing, one of the ruined. That I'm different."

She drew in a breath of air in a gasp. "No, they can't do that to you. You're not even old enough for Selection yet!"

"It doesn't matter. Once my genetics come back, they can do whatever they want. That doctor wants me done."

"Flynn, I want to do something. Tell me how to help you."

He shook his head and pulled away from her. "No, Dee. It's too dangerous. You have to promise me that you'll stay out of it. I shouldn't even have called you. Listen, thanks for what you did for me. You're the only good thing in this place."

As Flynn started to reach for his virtual wristband, Deirdre called out, "Flynn, don't go yet! We can figure something out."

But Flynn's eyes had started to water, and so he hit the button on his virtual wristband to end the call. Deirdre reached out to him again but his image winked out. She was left alone in the holo room, at a loss for what to do next.

Back in his quarantine cell, Flynn rolled over. And over again. Hours went by like that, but he just couldn't think of a way out...no matter how many times he turned things over in his head.

4

Voice 1: "Cancel the visit from your family. Listen, I found something in the IDream data transfer."

Voice 2: "What do you mean?"

Voice 1: "You know the artifact we've been seeing in the neurology reports? There's no artifact; it's functioning as designed. There is a pattern to the data, like a pulse. And it overstimulates the brain's sleep center. Look, no one knows about this, alright? But the transfer shuts down natural sleep rhythms."

Voice 2: "The IDreams cause insomnia?"

Voice 1: "Yeah. The more dreams you download, the more you want - because you can't sleep without them."

Voice 2: "We have to tell someone."

Voice 1: "Are you joking? You want us all to disappear? I am saving your family here. Don't tell anyone else about it, or we're through. Just tell your family you're sick or something. But whatever you do, cancel."

-Transcript of a phone call, IDream cloud archive,
June 15, 2050

That same morning, Antrim waited for Deirdre at the usual spot, the intersection of P and Q on Level 25. Antrim's background was a sad one; she had been orphaned at an early age. Her mother had fallen in love with an older man when she was just a girl and had given birth by the time she was 16. With the age difference between Antrim and her much older father, she had lost him to the descent over five years ago. A year after her father's descent, her mother had come down with cancer of the lungs.

It was heartbreaking, watching her mother slowly deteriorate after being hit with a radiation leak in the city's power station. The doctor had said that certain sacrifices for the city were necessary; someone had to be selected to keep the lights on. Antrim remembered her frightened mother holding her hand, pleading with her to be scheduled for the ritual before the end came. She was ready for Tír na nÓg. The doctor had made the arrangements, and then she was gone, taken away to whatever waited at the bottom of the city.

Something had shaken loose in Antrim after that. She became more fearful, less secure without the solid ground her parents had provided. These days, she lived with her uncle, Brandan O'Connor. He wasn't a man who took to children very easily, and Antrim thought of her friends as the only real family she had left. She clung to Deirdre, feeling a strength there that she thought she lacked. The moments spent on her board were her only unburdened ones.

Antrim's back was starting to hurt from leaning against the hard concrete for so long. She checked the time on her wristband device and saw that a message was coming through. It made a gentle ping and she she hit the receive button to start the message. Like a blue neon tickertape, the scrolling holographic letters moved from right to left, giving her about two seconds to read each word.

The message read, "I won't be coming to school today. Need to talk soon. -D."

Antrim sighed and pulled her expandable board out of her bag. Grabbing hold of the two edges, she enlarged it into an hourglass shape and popped out the anti-friction nodes. Then she let it drop to the floor where it hovered a few inches off the concrete. Antrim hopped onto her favorite ride and began to skate toward the lift that would take her to the school. Sailing past the air shaft, she took one peek down the channel that ran to the bottom of the city. She couldn't see much between the spinning fan blades but still she looked. Whispering, she said, "What happened to you down there, Ma and Da?"

Deirdre came out of her call with Flynn and lay for a moment in her top bunk. Turning over in bed, she still felt heavy from sleep and fatigue. Images of Flynn's 'Mare sentence and the argument with her father floated through her head. Yesterday had not been her best day. *There has to be a way to help him.*

Going to school after everything that had happened felt like too much. She activated her wristband and sent a ticker to Antrim that she wouldn't be meeting up with her. Then she rolled out of bed and dressed for the day without waking Breck. Tiptoeing to the bedroom door, she pulled it open and slipped out into the common room. To her surprise, she found both of her parents standing there, waiting. Deirdre stopped short, wondering why they weren't at the Academy already.

Siobhan walked over and put her arm around Deirdre's shoulders. She said, "Deirdre, the Ministry of Dream Justice has requested an interview with you this morning. You won't be going to school today."

"Ma, is this about what happened with me and Flynn yesterday?" she exclaimed. "I've already gone to detention and said I was sorry to the headmistress."

Siobhan shook her head. "No, daughter. It's about *Red Oak*. There's an investigation going on right now into the work Maeve was doing. Because she ran at the ritual."

Sean added, "Maeve helped your mother build *Red Oak*, and so your mother and I were interviewed yesterday at the Academy. Now the Ministry is interviewing everyone who has downloaded that dream. This morning we received a ticker that you will be interviewed next. You will go and answer their questions as honestly as you can. Do you understand what is being asked of you?"

Deirdre stepped backwards, feeling a little sick to her stomach. This meant she had made it onto the Ministry's list. But she wouldn't be vulnerable in front of her father, or show him that she was afraid. She looked hard at Sean and said, "So, that's it? The Ministry drops you a note and you just hand over your daughter on a plate? I'm not going."

Sean shook his head angrily and replied, "Deirdre, you don't have a choice. An interview has been scheduled with the Minister's Second and you must comply."

Deirdre turned toward her mother and said, "What about you, Ma? Are you just going to let Da take me away? He's worse than a Dream Drone. He's perfectly awake, yet he helps them in any way he can."

Siobhan ran her hands through her dark hair. "Daughter. Your father is right. Don't be so hard on him. You have to go."

Deirdre's hands tightened and her nails bit into her palms. She jerked her head up and said, "Ma! Are you joking? Do I have to remind you what happened the last time I was interviewed by the Ministry? You both told me to tell the truth. Now Zinna...well, she won't ever be the same since her dreamlock and what happened in that 'Mare. And I put her there."

Siobhan said, "Deirdre, she was the one hiding contraband. Not you. Why should you be punished or take her place? You're too important."

"I'm not important. And I could have said something else. Something to throw them off! And now you want me to face them all over again. I won't go. Ma, why won't you ever stand up to Father? If ever there was a time to stand in between me and him, it's now. But you're too weak, aren't you?"

Siobhan lowered her eyes to the floor and said, "We love you, Deirdre."

But Deirdre couldn't stop; she was too angry. Pointing at her mother she said, "No, you don't. Or you wouldn't let this happen. I don't ever want to be like you, Ma."

Siobhan turned away and walked into the bedroom, closing the door behind her.

Sean, however, was not as easily cowed as his wife. He yelled with all the force of a Master Maker, "Deirdre, that's enough!" She was startled into silence, and he continued, "You will show your mother respect, and not speak to her that way. You will also show the interviewer respect, and if I hear otherwise you will regret it. We are leaving, now!"

Breck poked her head out of the bedroom, hair still tousled from dream. She asked, "What is going on out here?"

Deirdre and Sean ignored her and left their unit in a fragile silence. They walked to the lift, both of them just staring straight ahead. Deirdre felt betrayed on all sides; she wondered if she had the two worst parents in the city. They entered the lift on Level 28 and Sean pressed the button that would take them up to Level 1. It was a long, uncomfortable ride up to the section of the city that housed the administrative arm of Dream Justice. The Dream Justice building extended above ground and provided an operational base for the Minister and his top administrators. Deirdre's interview was to take place in one of the below ground rooms - she didn't have access privileges for the surface, and so they had to accommodate her restrictions.

They stepped off the lift on the first level of the city to the muted sound of doors sliding open. Deirdre could smell a hint of the sea drifting through the hallways and hungered to know what Topside was really like. *But I won't find out today.* She followed her father through the twists and turns of the brightly lit hallways. She was a little surprised that he knew the section so well; she thought he spent most of his time over at the Academy with the other Makers.

The section where the interview was to be held was filled with Dream Drones who guarded every identity checkpoint. Over and over she heard, "Sean Callaghan. Deirdre Callaghan. Identity Confirmed," as they passed through each pair of metal pillars flanking every major doorway. Watchful red gargoyles, they allowed no one to pass without consent. Deirdre had been through plenty of scanners before, but never so many on one level. She knew that the scanners transmitted her father's identity from his weaver profile to the cloud, where the location was checked against his access privileges. Her own identity was verified through her earbud device.

Finally, they passed through the last checkpoint where two Dream Drones waited to escort them to the interview room. Deirdre's palms were starting to feel a little slippery from n erves. They reached the doorway to room 1402, and her father prepared to enter with her. But the Drone extended his arm against Sean's chest and refused him admittance. He said, "Maker Callaghan. You will need to wait here. Only interviewees beyond this po int."

Sean nodded curtly and stepped back. Deirdre felt nothing but contempt for him. *Good morning, Dream Drone. I'm here to hand over my oldest daughter. Can I lick your boots now?* The Drone put his hand on the back of Deirdre's elbow, and angled her forward into the interview room. He wasn't just trying to direct her where to go, he was also making sure that she didn't turn around and make a run for it. Deirdre let herself be escorted. *What can they need to ask me that is so bloody important?* When the door shut behind her, blocking the only exit, she felt a lot less sure of herself.

The room was empty except for a man, two chairs, and a table. The man was seated in one of the chairs, and the other chair waited empty for her. The Second was dressed all in red and she remembered him from Maeve's ritual, a large man in a crisp uniform. Her eyes were drawn to the spider insignia near the collar and she swallowed hard. She hated that that image and dreaded being fitted for a weaver. She sat down in the chair and tried to keep her breath even.

The man in front of her sat quietly, studying a holographic display that had been projected onto the surface of the table. A few minutes went by with him ignoring her completely. *Am I in the right room?* Then he finally used the touch function and brought up a file with her name on it. He said, "This interview is being recorded. State your name for the archive record."

Deirdre cleared her throat and replied, "Deirdre Callaghan."

Briskly, he replied, "Thank you. My name is Dyl an O'Brian, and you will address me as Mr. O'Brian. I function as the

Minister's Second-in-command. Do you understand what that means?" He finally looked her in the eye.

Deirdre replied, "It means that the subject of this interview is important."

With a sly smile, Dylan replied, "Very good. You're the daughter of two Makers, I expected you to be intelligent. Now, if you want things to go well for you, please continue to be intelligent. Answer my questions exactly as I pose them to you. Do you understand?"

As emotionlessly as possible, Deirdre replied, "Yes, I understand."

Looking back down at his data file, Dylan continued, "Good. Now I see from the records on the cloud that you accessed the dream called *Red Oak* on 9.12.77 and 9.13.77. You spent a total time in that dream of 20 hours of lived experience. This is an inquiry about *Red Oak*. Tell me what you experienced in dream."

Deirdre hesitated for a moment, remembering Maeve's words. *Tell no one of Roenin.* She didn't know if Dylan knew about the black warrior, and it would be a risk not to name him. But Maeve had spent the last moments of her life giving her that warning. So she said, "Yes, I downloaded *Red Oak* on those occasions. I walked through an oak tree forest in autumn. And there was a castle where a woman lived."

Dylan took notes with a stylus as she spoke. Looking back up, he prodded her, "Yes. Anything else?"

Still Deirdre felt that she had to protect the secret of Roenin, whatever it was. She said, "Oh yes. I forgot. There was a fighter, dressed in grey, practicing with his staff."

Dylan paused and just stared at her. Deirdre looked him straight in the eye and again kept her face as empty as a still pond. *He's trying to make me reveal myself in some misstep. But it's not going to work.*

Finally, Dylan broke eye contact. He said, "All right, Miss Callaghan. Thank you for your cooperation. Your description of *Red Oak* matches that of other beta dreamers who have tested that content: a warrior, a castle, a woman, and a forest. Access to *Red Oak* will be terminated from this point forward. I look forward to the day of your Selection and learning how you will serve the

Ministry. You are excused. The Ministry provides." Then he put his stylus in his chest pocket, logged out of the data file on the cloud, and promptly left the room.

Deirdre remained seated for a moment, feeling a little dizzy. She had eluded one of the top administrators of Dream Justice, and she felt a little drunk on the rush of it. She placed her sweaty palms flat on the table to steady herself. She hadn't told him about Roenin. And none of the other dreamers had seen him. *But how is that possible? Sure, you can explore a dream. But the content - the main characters and the world - don't change from dreamer to dreamer. The Makers set up the rules of the world from the beginning. Could Maeve have told all of the beta testers not to mention him? Unlikely. She barely managed to tell me in her last moments. So that means Roenin only appeared to me, which is so strange. I talked with him. Watched him fight. We took the castle. It doesn't make any sense.*

Deirdre rubbed her eyes. She wasn't going to get any answers sitting in Dream Justice. *He was so real. Maybe the most intense character I have ever met in dream. Maeve and mother, what have you built? Well, it doesn't matter now. Whatever it is, will have to wait.* Outside in the hallway, her father was waiting. He waved her over and together they walked out of Dream Justice.

"You did well in there, daughter," he said. "Dylan was impressed with how you carried yourself."

"Thanks, Da," she replied. "I told him everything I know."

Breck hurried from school as fast as the excess of people in the hallways would allow. She had an outing planned with her mother that she couldn't miss. Today Siobhan would go to the Spinners and retrieve her Offering jumper. Breck had insisted on going, and Siobhan had promised. So she used her slim frame to squeeze between the people in the hallways, darting home as fast as possible.

She smiled happily to herself as she rounded the last corner to her home and burst through the doorway. "Ma, I'm back," she exclaimed, loud enough to wake Tír na nÓg.

"There you are," said her mother, peering from around her Sequencer. "Just one moment. I need to finish this bit."

"Ma! You've been working on that forever. C'mere! We have to go."

Siobhan looked at her youngest from top to toe and said, "My, my. Someone is excited to go and see the Spinners." As Breck pouted, Siobhan made one last adjustment.

Not letting up, Breck pointed to her mother and said, "I'm here on time. You promised we would go today, and you promised I could come."

Siobhan stood, arranged her clothing, and pushed her long black hair away from her face. Once a glorious mane, it was now brittle and showing streaks of grey. "When you get a little older, Breck, you will understand better why those in their fourth decade aren't excited to visit the Spinners." She sighed and said, "Alright, let's be on our way." Siobhan shooed Breck out the door and locked the sliding entrance to their unit.

As they walked to the lift, Breck said, "Ma, everyone at school says that the Spinners know things, like what your Selection will be and what life will be like in the Tír na nÓg."

Siobhan adjusted the sleeves on her robe and said, "Yes, daughter, those are the stories that are whispered in the hallways of our city."

"Then I'm going to ask ours all kinds of questions. Even if she does smell a little like the ruined."

Siobhan placed her arm on her daughter's shoulder. "Though she is an older woman, we must show respect. I am even older than her, remember? I will tell you what I have heard." Siobhan leaned in with a conspiratorial look in her eyes. In a softer voice, she said, "The Spinners never take husbands and never have children, but their apprentices are like their daughters. It is said that Spinners know yarns and fibers so intimately, that they can look at a strand of your hair and tell you your future."

And with that last word almost a whisper, Siobhan reached quietly around her daughter's waist and surprised her with a hail of tickles. But their laughter stopped short as a Dream Drone turned the corner. Laughter was not something that you heard often in Skellig City. Siobhan tucked her hands inside her orange Maker robes and nodded to the Drone. Breck looked down at the floor and fell into step slightly behind her mother.

The Drone nodded back, "Maker."

"The Ministry provides," responded Siobhan, and they hurried onward before the Drone decided that they were worth more attention. Both mother and daughter were thankful when the boot steps of the Drone faded behind them.

Siobhan said, "Of course none of it is true. What is said about the Spinners and the future."

Breck said, "Well, I'm going to ask ours anyway."

The remainder of the trip was silent. Breck busied herself following the patterns in the walkway floor as they made their way to the level that housed the Spinners. Over the years, the concrete floors had been painted in various shades of grey, some warm and some cool. The center of the walkway had been worn down to bare concrete by the many thousands of steps that were taken every day by the residents of the city. But at the edges, the different paint colors formed a patchwork of worn paint chips. Under years of abuse, the paint was hanging on by sheer force of will.

After taking the lift to Level 35, Siobhan and Breck arrived in the domain of the Spinners. The entrance to their section was marked by unusual textiles in fabulous colors which were not seen anywhere else in the city. A large burgundy tapestry of delicate workmanship hung in the center of the walkway, split down the middle for people to pass. Siobhan stepped through first and held the fabric apart for Breck. The space the Spinners created was like another world.

Passing along the hallway, they walked among more hanging tapestries, quilts, and knitted panels. Siobhan explained that it was a gallery of sorts where apprentices displayed their work for critique by the more experienced women. As they made their way deeper into the section, one of the apprentices, a girl of 18 years, approached. She was dressed in the winter-white floor-length tunic of the Spinners. Their dress symbolized their most important work: producing tunics of the same shade for every person who entered the cylinder. For everyone in Skellig City, white was the color of the dead.

"Greetings, Siobhan," the girl said. "Your time approaches. I see that you are here for your ritual clothing. This way. I believe that Spinner Niamh finished your garment this week." Beckoning, she led them onward through the labyrinth of hallways in which the Spinners made their home. Following quickly, Breck gaped at all of the beautifully colored fabrics that adorned the walls and floors.

When they reached the workspace for her mistress, the apprentice bowed her head and said, "Spinner Niamh, the Offering has arrived to speak with you."

The room was filled with woven bags that held every color of yarn and thread that could be produced by the dyeing vats of Skellig City. It was a priceless amount of yarn, used only for the making of textile art by the Spinners. No livestock was kept in Skellig City, and new yarn was made by a careful process of taking apart old strands and spinning them into new yarn to be dyed and worked. The bags were lined up in order from red to blue; a rainbow of color stretched along the walls.

Spinner Niamh looked up from a large wooden loom at the center of the room. There she was working on a large tapestry in twenty shades of green. "Ah, Siobhan," said the Spinner. "I see you've brought your youngest one. I have your ritual jumper over here." She stood up slowly, stretching out her back before taking a step. She walked with a hunch, no doubt created from a lifetime of bending over threadwork.

Mother and daughter followed her to a room at the back of the workspace. This new room was filled with nothing but winter-white yarn. The Spinner moved slowly toward the room's worktable; her joints feeling the burden of her 34 years.

The apprentice rushed forward. "Here, Niamh. Let me. You sit."

The Spinner replied stubbornly, "Yes. Yes. Why do you have to fuss so?"

The apprentice smiled indulgently and helped the Spinner into her chair before the worktable. Then the young apprentice said to Siobhan, "She is even more infirm than her years suggest.

But that is because you won't see the doctors, isn't that right, Niamh?"

Turning to Breck, the Spinner said, "The doctors will take away my ability to See. Ignore that one. She is only trying to get me in trouble. Now, Breck. Do you see this chair? In it, I have knitted patterns to bring over 100 people to their descent and beyond to Tír na nÓg. But I won't be around to make yours. My saddest day was when I had to start on my own. So much work unfinished."

The apprentice went to the table and began to unfold Siobhan's ritual jumper. The Callaghan family pattern was a basic seed stitch until you reached a large center knot at the center of the chest. It was beautiful, but Siobhan couldn't bring herself to touch it. Breck reached out to it instead, running her fingers along the intricate knot at the center.

The Spinner said, "You see its beauty, pretty one. Let me show you the Book of Patterns. Sit on the edge of my chair if you can."

Breck gasped with excitement; there was only one book allowed in the city and it belonged to the Spinners. She eased herself gently onto the Spinner's chair and tried to ignore the woman's smell. From the shelf behind the chair, the Spinner pulled out a large square object and placed it into her hands. It was covered on both sides with soft green cloth, and seams were sewn into one side to hold the whole thing together. The Spinner reached forward and pulled away the section of cloth that covered one side. Underneath was a picture.

The apprentice said, "Spinner, no!" But Niamh waved her aside.

Breck stared at the picture. It was a miniature landscape scene of fluffy white animals on green land bounded by stone fences. An earthen covered hut was on the highest hillside. The sky was thread stitched over paint in a light, cobalt-blue silk, and it even shimmered in the low light.

Breck said, "This is a picture. But it doesn't move like the pictures in dreams."

Spinner Niamh ran her fingers across the green hills and stonework fences on the cover of the book. "Once there was a place like this. A place that moved all of the time. Because it was real

86

and alive. And because the things that lived fulfilled their own purpose, a purpose that no one had to set for them. This land was filled with growing things, and a tiny spark of magic in each one helped it to find its way. The old country, it was called. And there were other creatures. Special creatures that were made entirely of magic. The banshee and the pooka were two of the fae that hid in the hills. Look close. Do you see any of them?"

Breck looked hard but she couldn't see anything. "Are you making up a story, Spinner Niamh?"

Then the apprentice interjected, "Yes, Breck, she is. There was no land like this. Spinner, show her the patterns or I will take the book away. And you won't find it as easily as last time."

The Spinner shot her a hard look but began turning the pages for Breck. The book was filled with knitting pattern after knitting pattern, all alphabetized by family name. She turned to the fibrous pages to the "C" section, and Breck saw the Callaghan knot.

"There we are, mother," Breck said. She turned to look at the eyes of the Spinner, one white from a cataract and the other a blinding blue. "Spinner Niamh," she began timidly. "Do you think you could tell me my future?"

The aging woman chuckled with a deep phlegmy laugh. "I can try, dear. Doesn't everyone want to know their destiny? What is your question?"

"I want to know...I want to know if the city can love me. Like they love the Dream Match girls."

Siobhan drew in a breath and murmured, "No, Breck."

But the Spinner didn't notice. She said, "It always comes down to love of some sort. But first, I need to find out more about you."

Breck slid herself back onto the floor, and the Spinner plucked one curling auburn hair from her head. She asked, "What do you look at my hair for, Spinner?"

The woman said, "Oh, I search out the life force of someone in how the hair turns in the light, its color, and its texture. Then I think deeply on that person, pondering her life and what it will hold. There are as many futures as there are choices in the world. Out of all of those possible futures, I have to see the one where magic is the strongest. Many futures, but only one true path. Yes."

The Spinner closed her eyes and began to rock slightly back and forth in her chair, holding Breck's hair lightly in one hand. With eyes closed, she began to hum the notes of an old folk tune; the words of which had been long forgotten. Breck shifted her weight from one foot to the other and clasped her hands.

Then, in an instant, the old woman sat up straight, as stiff as the back of the chair in which she sat. Her eyes fluttered beneath closed lids and she tilted her head back toward the ceiling. Niamh began speaking in a clear, lilting voice, as if the last 20 years had dropped from her body.

> *"Two stars burning bright*
> *Sisters shining through the night*
> *One will stay and one will go*
> *Shadow covers those who know.*
>
> *One turns dark, the other light*
> *One eats the moon with all its might*
> *A war will come and it will show*
> *The dreams that punish those made low."*

The Spinner then fell silent and her body began to shake as if in seizure. Breck backed away quickly, pressing herself into the table. The apprentice and Siobhan darted forward to the Spinner, trying to hold her upper body still as the shaking became worse.

Siobhan looked in the eyes of the apprentice and said, "Her weaver must be malfunctioning!"

The apprentice ignored her and snapped at Breck in clipped words. "What have you done?"

Breck exclaimed, "I didn't do anything!"

The apprentice said, "Take your garment and go, Siobhan. Go! Get out already!"

Stricken, Siobhan grabbed her knitted jumper in one hand and Breck's hand with the other. Together, they ran from the Spinners, only slowing as they reached the lift and hit the call button.

Breathing heavily, Breck asked, "Ma, what was that? What happened back there?"

"Breck," Siobhan said, "I want you to forget everything that woman said."

"But Ma, who is the star shining bright?"

Siobhan said, "Breck! Listen to me. Forget everything, do you hear? Your life may someday depend on it."

Breck nodded, but she knew there was no way that she could stop thinking about what had just happened. The words of the Spinner would weigh on her mind until she found some sense in them.

They came for him early in the morning. Flynn heard gruff men's voices and roused himself from a sleepless night. He pulled his sore body to a sitting position as the Medical Director and his two assistants approached his cell. Odran was dressed in his usual lab coat, and his men were dressed in shorter white jackets.

Stopping in front of the barrier, the scientist examined Flynn closely. "Waking up from a restful sleep? I think not," he said slyly. "No sleeping without the Protocol to put you under, yes? Our brilliant founder saw to that centuries ago."

Flynn walked over to the barrier and said, "Yeah, well. I'll be sure to look him up in Tír na nÓg to say thanks."

The Director said, "That you may. And soon, I hear. Now stand away from the barrier, lad. We have tests to complete today."

Flynn looked him in the eyes, crossed his arms, and just stood there.

"Very well," said Odran. "Computer. Sequentially reduce size of quarantine area. Execute."

The electrostatic barrier began to glow on all four walls in Flynn's cell. He took a step back from the Director and the barrier winked out, appearing a half second later and one foot closer on all sides.

Flynn shouted, "Are you trying to cut me in half?"

The Director just shrugged. The barrier winked out again and Flynn backed up even more. This time it reappeared even closer on all sides. Half a minute later, Flynn was standing in a two-foot-square area at the center of his cell. He balled his fists up at his sides and glared at Odran.

The Director motioned to his two assistants. "Go get him and strap him down on the exam table." The two burly assistants smiled wickedly and started towards Flynn.

Flynn put his fists up and launched a punch as soon as the barrier was down. But what the assistants lacked between the ears was made up for in muscle and sinew. The one on the left dodged Flynn's punch while the other one came up from behind. He threw his arms around Flynn's chest, pinning his arms and hoisting him up. Flynn tried to kick out with his feet, but the other assistant quickly grabbed his legs.

Letting out a growl, Flynn said, "Blast it! Let go of me, you morons."

Ignoring Flynn's protests, they carried him like a rolled carpet over to the exam table. Flynn kept struggling while the two brutes strapped him down, fastening straps around his wrists, ankles, and neck. When he was secure, Odran came closer, wheeling over his prize piece of medical tech that would evaluate Flynn's symptoms. It was shaped like a blinking half-donut with a hole in the center where Flynn's body would slide through.

The Director positioned the device over Flynn's head and then reached for a syringe to draw his blood. He said, "First, I'm taking your blood for the genetic defect panel." Odran selected the fattest needle in his red kit and screwed it onto the syringe.

Flynn grimaced as the needle punched through a vein in his arm and sucked out his blood.

"So many medical advances," said Odran, holding the filled syringe up to the light. "But there's still no substitute for fresh blood."

Flynn grunted and looked the other way.

"Next we're going to put the medical scanner to work." Odran snapped his fingers and one assistant stepped forward with a plastic cup of viscous white liquid. The burly man held the cup up to Flynn's lips while the other one pulled his head back, ensuring that Flynn would drink. Flynn opened his mouth and slurped the liquid, pretending to comply. Once the cup was empty, he spat it out into the Director's face. The white liquid congealed on the end of his nose and looked quite disgusting.

Odran gave no response, but closed his eyes and pulled a handkerchief out of his pocket. He wiped his face and finally said, "We have other methods. This can be as difficult as you like." He snapped again and the other assistant came forward with a flexible plastic tube. Flynn struggled again, but together the assistants stuffed the tube down his throat. One minute later, Flynn's stomach was full of the white liquid. He coughed and sputtered as they drew out the tube.

The Director brought up the controls on the medical scanner and activated the machine. The multi-colored lights along the edges blinked faster and the machine hummed slightly as it took Flynn's readings. Odran read the scan results aloud. "Let's see, Flynn. You show tissue breakdown in the skin, hair, joints, and heart. Cause? Hmm. Immune markers are dangerously high. And there we have it. Your body is attacking itself, and the decay of ageing is the result. Excellent."

Flynn coughed out, "I'm not old. I'm 15; you can check my birth records!"

Again the Director ignored his protests. "Once I confirm the genetic defect with your blood, I'll have all the evidence I need."

Flynn pushed against the restraints and pleaded, "I can live and work until I'm 35, just like anybody else."

The Director shut down the scanner and shook his head. "And pass along your defect to your progeny? I won't allow it." He turned to the assistants and said, "Toss him back in quarantine. We're through here." Then he checked a ticker message on his wristband and swept from the clinic.

Flynn was manhandled back to his cage and shoved to the floor. The two men backed out, and the barrier re-activated itself. Flynn lay still on the floor, waiting for the two of them to leave. Then he forced himself up on his knees and vomited until all of the thick white fluid was out of him. He wiped his face with his sleeve and pulled himself onto his metal bed.

Like he had done before, he rolled over, covered his face with an arm, and placed a holo call to Deirdre. In a few moments, they were together, in a virtual space sized for two people. Flynn imagined himself like he felt, and he felt terrible.

Deirdre blinked in shock when she saw him. She reached out as if to touch him, and then drew her hand back. "Flynn. What happened? Are you hurt? You look sick."

"I'm sorry to call you again, Dee. I really shouldn't have. I just...I just feel so low." Flynn spat on the floor and coughed some more.

"Tell me. What is happening in there?"

Flynn rubbed his sleeve across his mouth. "He's doing just what he said he'd do. Running tests till he gets his evidence. It won't be long for me now, Dee."

"But Flynn, what if your tests came back normal? What then?"

With downturned lips he looked at her and said, "You know they won't."

"But if the Ministry looked up the results in the cloud - the official record - and the results were normal. Wouldn't they have to let you go?"

Flynn shrugged and said, "I guess so." Then his eyes widened and he stood a little straighter. "Wait a minute, Dee. I know you. You're working something out. I told you not to get involved."

Deirdre raised her wristband and placed her finger on the control that would end her connection to the room. "Remember the other day when we were walking to school, and that man ran by? You told me about that dream where you were UNDER GROUND. Well, I'm going to download it."

Flynn put together what she meant and said, "Dee, no..." But it was too late - she hit the disconnect button and was gone. Flynn kicked the wall, and it bounced under the impact like rubber. He shouted, "Blast it! Why are you so hard-headed, Deirdre Callaghan? You never listen to anyone!" He kicked the wall again; a little softer this time. "You turn everything upside down!" Then he slid to the floor and rested his head on his knees. To himself he whispered "Why do I care about you so? My impossible girl."

Deirdre came out of the holo call knowing what she had to do. Using her earbud she logged onto the public directory in the cloud and searched for Cashel Quinn. She learned quickly that he was assigned to the night shift for wastewater treatment. *He'll be coming home just as everyone else is leaving for the day - and I know right where to find him.*

In her bedroom she wrapped herself in Flynn's cloak and gave herself a check in the mirror. She tied her hair back in a ponytail and brought the hood up over her head. Then she took the remaining loose cloth and threw it over her shoulder, obscuring her face like she had seen Flynn do a hundred times. Now she could pass for either gender, and no one would recognize her as a Callaghan. *Today, I'm going to find the underground, and they're going to help us. No matter what.*

She tiptoed out of bedroom and crept to the door. Hitting the controls to open it, she peeked left and right. The hallway was empty, so she headed out, her knapsack hidden under the loose folds of grey wool. She entered the lift and stepped off on Level 25, heading for the intersection of P and Q sections. She walked casually, like a person that belonged, and resisted the urge to look over her shoulder. Pausing at the intersection, she checked her wristband for the time. *It's 8:00, so he should be coming up here any minute.*

She decided to cruise around the section in a loop, hoping to catch sight of him in the hallway on his way home. Around to the lift and back past his unit she walked, all the while putting together her plan. *The Medical Director can't schedule the descent on his own. He has to convince someone in Dream Justice. What if just as he is making his case, the data changes and says Flynn is normal? That could work, right?*

On her second loop, she saw him. Cashel Quinn, the man with the ponytail, stepped off the lift. Deirdre was already behind him, so he was easy to follow. He paused for a moment at his doorway while the system confirmed his access profile. The door slid open and he stepped inside. Deirdre quickened her steps to the door and heard the click of Drone boots coming from around the corner. She slipped through and out of sight right before it closed and locked. She was in.

She stood still, her eyes adjusting to the lower light in his living room. The space was unremarkable, and was laid out like any other unit she had been in before. There was a sitting area in the main room and two doors: one for the bathroom and one for the bedroom. A few empty Nutripaks and some dirty clothes littered the room; the man was not tidy. For a moment, Deirdre's confidence faltered. The place just looked so ordinary. *What if he isn't underground like Flynn thought?*

Cashel walked out of the bathroom, saw her standing there, and stopped short. Then he threw himself into motion. Lunging for a chair on the left, he hoisted it, and prepared to throw it. "By the Minister's moustache, what are you doing in here?"

Deirdre dropped her hood and said, "Just hold on! I'm not Ministry, and I'm here to talk to you. I need help from the underground."

Cashel lowered the chair and snorted, "Just a kid, eh?" Then he turned away from her. In two long strides he was in the kitchen, and grabbed his dinner out of the cupboard. "Get out of here, little girl," he said. "This isn't for you."

Deirdre frowned and her eyes narrowed. She said, "I'm not a little girl. And I'll get out when you agree to help me. My friend is in trouble."

"A lot of people in this city are in trouble. Do you see me helping them?" Cashel pushed some clothes out of the way and sat down on the couch.

Deirdre walked over to stand in front of him. *Time to bluff.* "I know your name, where you live, and where you work. I also know what you do in your spare time."

The man stuck a straw into his Nutripak and started drinking. After two slurps he cocked his head to the side and asked, "And what is that?"

Pointing at him, Deirdre said, "You're part of a network of people committed to sabotaging the Ministry. You hack into the cloud. You steal dreams and sell them for information and favors.

You want the Minister destroyed. But if you don't help me, I'm going to turn you in to the next Drone I see."

Cashel sat a little straighter on the couch and was silent for a few breaths. Then he leaned back again and said, "Alright, Deirdre Callaghan. You think you know me. But I know you too. You're a Maker's daughter. So, what is it like at the top of the food chain?"

"What is it like working with the underground?"

"Oh, I wouldn't know. I'm just a man at the bottom in wastewater treatment."

Deirdre took a deep breath and let it out in frustration as Cashel calmly slurped his Nutripak again. She said, "We're on the same side. My friend is captured, and they're going to kill him if we don't help."

"Hypothetically speaking, what is it that you think I can do for your friend? Take out the entire Drone army?"

"I'm being serious. My friend has an ageing disorder and they're calling him ruined. I need a data profile to show that his lab work is normal. I need a way to upload it to the medical archive. And I need to know when the Medical Director is meeting with Dylan O'Brian."

"Just that?" Cashel gave a snort and then took another slurp on his Nutripak.

Deirdre said, "If you're really underground, it shouldn't be hard. And if you're not underground...well, I doubt that the Drones I talk to will care. There are Dream Justice quotas and I am a Maker's daughter, after all. At the top of the food chain."

Cashel got off the couch and spread his arms wide. "Well, little girl, I'm willing to gamble that you're not going to turn me in. If you do, how will you save your friend? So, I propose a different kind of relationship. Fee for service." He took another drink from the Nutripak.

"I see," said Deirdre, crossing her arms over her chest. "And what do you want as payment?"

Cashel's face turned into a smile and his full lips let go of the straw. "A Dream Maker's Sequencer."

Deirdre's jaw dropped open slightly. "A Sequencer! You've got to be kidding."

"If you're really a Maker's daughter, it shouldn't be hard," he quipped, mirroring the tone of voice she had used on him a moment ago.

"Fine," she said. "You'll have it first thing tomorrow. But my data better be here."

"Sure thing, sweetheart. A deal is a deal."

"Just so you know, I expected you to be different," Deirdre said, preparing to leave. "My opinion of the underground has gone way down."

"Whatever, lass. Fill out a survey. See you on the morrow."

Deirdre brought up her hood, wrapped the cloak around her face once more, and left the room. She walked back to the lift on Level 25 but barely noticed anything along the way. *How am I going to steal a Sequencer from my parents?*

Flynn sat on the floor of his cell, staring at the wall. He silently counted the tiles opposite to where he sat. Again. His eyes were puffy and dark underneath from sleeplessness. The Medical Director was nearby, sitting at his workstation in the main area. He reviewed pages of text and spoke softly to himself at odd intervals.

Flynn glanced over at the Director and said, "What are you doing?"

Odran paused the scrolling data and looked up from his work. "Assembling my report in your medical file."

"My results are back, then?"

"Oh yes. They came in this morning. I have your defect here, a fault on chromosome 14."

Flynn turned away, his face wrinkled in disgust. "Good for you," he said bitterly.

"Yes, good for me," said the Director. "Tomorrow I meet with the Minister's Second and give my recommendations." He turned back to his work.

Flynn's breathing quickened, coming in shallow gasps. His eyes narrowed to a squint and he studied the Director. Then he stood up, his breath now coming in heaves. Still the Director ignored him. So Flynn let out a yell and ran at the barrier, ramming his shoulder into the invisible field. The barrier repelled him with equal force, letting out a sharp snap of electricity. It threw him back onto the floor and he slid along the slick tiles, coming to a stop at the opposite wall. The impact had hit him hard and he struggled to stand up again, pulling at the wall for support.

Odran finally looked up and said, "Don't hurt yourself, lad. I plan to make an example of you for the entire city, and I need the goods to be intact. This will be a descent that everyone attends."

Flynn leaned on the wall and stared at the Director with hatred in his eyes. In a soft voice he said, "You don't get to decide who lives and who doesn't."

Odran stood up from the table and closed down his cloud access. He said, "Maybe not. But I know the people that do." Then he strode from the room, a man consumed.

5

Janice: Can't believe u get to vaca @ Skellig Cty
Resort. Wish I was.

Laurie: I no. Mum says the dreams r killer. Bt
mostly she wants her besty 2 b jealous.

Janice: How did u get on the list?

Laurie: Da contracts 4 IDream shipping engine
parts. Ther buildng somthng big.

Janice: Wht?

Laurie: Who cares? As long as I get 2 go.

- Text message exchange
Date stamp 4.22.2048

Deirdre was awake in bed, staring at the ceiling. She could hear Breck's slow, regular breathing in the bunk below. In the dark of the room, she raised her wristband over her face and checked the time. *Two AM. Time to go.*

She pulled back the wool covers slowly and eased her legs over the edge of the mattress until her feet found the rungs of the ladder. Breck's sleeping didn't change at all, so Deirdre dropped to the floor without making a sound. *She's dreaming deeply tonight. Good.*

Once in the common area, she went to her parents' bedroom door and paused there, listening against the gap. The only sound coming from the room was her father's snoring. She stood there listening for a long time. Just listening. Her fingers began to tingle because somewhere along the way she had stopped breathing. Forcing a deep breath, she closed her eyes. *This is for Flynn. That's all that matters.*

She pushed the door open just far enough to squeeze through. A sliver of greenish light from the emergency bulb in the kitchen fell across her parents' sleeping bodies. Still, her father's snoring didn't change. *Which one should I take? He's the one that's helping them the most. So his.* Slowly she crept over to the foot of her parents' bed where a chest of drawers was placed against the wall. Deirdre knew that the drawers were divided the way her parents slept. Her father always took the left side of the bed, so she reached for the top drawer on the left.

Slowly, so slowly, she pulled her father's Sequencer out. But the movement of metal against metal gave out a high-pitched squeak. Sean's snoring stopped and Deirdre went completely still, her fingers resting lightly on the prize. She stopped breathing again and stayed that way until her father rolled over and the snoring resumed. *I've got to get out of here.*

She wrapped her fingers around the Sequencer and pulled it out, being careful not to bump it on anything. Stowing it under her arm, she lifted and slid the drawer back into place without making any more noise. With her objective in hand, she turned back to the door and tiptoed toward the light.

Just as she was about to disappear around the corner, her mother spoke. Siobhan sat up in bed and said, "Deirdre. I trust you to do the right thing. I always have, and I always will."

Deirdre looked back into the room at the sound of her mother's voice. The words and the loving tone in them caught her. The light from the kitchen fell across Siobhan's face and she saw her mother's dark eyes shining back at her. She wanted to say something, but somehow she just couldn't. The argument over her interview with the Second was still too fresh.

Siobhan whispered, "Goodnight, daughter." She then lay back down next to Sean.

Deirdre closed the door behind her and made it back to her own bunk. She stuffed the stolen Sequencer under her pillow and pulled the covers up over herself. Her mother's words felt paralyzing. *I am doing the right thing, aren't I?* She shook her head to clear her mind and set her alarm for 5:00 AM, early enough for her to leave the house before her father woke up.

Deirdre tossed and turned in her bed as the hours passed by. She didn't want to sleep; she wanted to keep thinking about how to break Flynn out of medical. Finally, she snapped alert to the sound of her wristband alarm going off. Pulling her tired body out of bed, she was eager to get out of the house before her father woke up and discovered the theft. She wrapped herself in Flynn's cloak again and stuffed the Sequencer into her knapsack underneath. A few minutes later, she was on Level 25 knocking on Cashel's door.

The door slid open and Cashel waved her inside. Deirdre's nose wrinkled – somehow the place smelled even worse than before. The odor of unwashed clothes and sweat was hard to take. Cashel looked a mess, too. Rumpled strands of hair had sneaked out of his ponytail, and puffy circles had developed under his eyes. It looked like he hadn't slept since she last saw him.

Deirdre cleared her throat and said, "Well. Are you finished?"

Cashel raised his eyebrows. "I'm finished, as long as you brought what I asked for."

Deirdre nodded and reached under her cloak for the knapsack. She went over to the table to sit it down and gently pulled out the Sequencer. She said, "Alright. Here's my part. Now where's yours?"

Cashel let out a soft whistle when she handed the Sequencer to him. He said, "Back in a minute." Cashel took the Sequencer into the other room and came back with something small in his hand. He held it out to her; in his palm was a shimmering blue orb, almost like an egg. It caught hints all of the colors in the room, almost like her glo ball from class. "Here is the data you need, love."

Deirdre took it gently in her hand and said, "It's beautiful. What is it?"

"Why it's a bug, of course, designed to deliver the data you need. A dragonfly, to be specific."

"A real dragonfly?"

"Well, no. But as real as it gets in this place. All the data on it is formatted to look like actual medical records and lab tests, complete with the Director's electronic signature. I even threw in a bonus and wrote a report stating that Flynn is normal. Now, when you get to the Director's desk on the medical unit..."

Deirdre interrupted him, saying, "Wait. What do you mean, his desk on the unit? I don't have to actually go there, do I? The place is guarded by Drones and who knows what else."

"Sorry, lass. Actually you do."

"No. Just stop. I thought you were some tech wizard. Don't you understand what cloud means?"

Cashel pulled out a chair and sat down at the table. "Yes, dearie. I know what cloud means. And you're almost not worth a Sequencer, by the way. Going through the cloud means that any data transfer will be logged along the network checkpoints. No way to get around that. Bad for you, and bad for your friend. You need to be physically at the Director's access point."

"No other way?"

Cashel shook his head and crossed his arms. "Nope. Not if you want the transfer to be invisible."

Deirdre closed her eyes in frustration. Exasperated, she sighed and said, "Whatever. Once I get in there, what do I do then?"

Cashel said, "First you activate the access portal in the desk and bring up the login screen. But do not try to type a password. This is important. Do you understand?"

"Yes. No password. Go on."

"Then, you hold the bug up to the portal," said Cashel, pointing at the orb in Deirdre's hands. "You blow on it softly to activate it. It will bloom and transmit a malware app through the access portal. It eats Flynn's entire data file, vomits out a new one, and then eats itself. No record. I'm keeping this simple so you can follow along."

She said, "Funny. You're almost not worth saving Flynn's life, by the way. And when it's finished? What do I do with it?"

"You'll find out."

Deirdre put the device into her sack. "Oh, all right. When is the Medical Director meeting with Dylan?"

Cashel pursed his lips and tilted his head to the side. "That's the bad news. The meeting is today at 3:00."

"What! Today?" Deirdre cried, her eyes wide with alarm.

Cashel shrugged. "That's the intel. I don't grind the sausage, I just deliver it. You and your friend have 7 hours to get this done."

Seven hours! I don't even know how to get in there yet. Deirdre quickly wrapped the cloak around her face again and walked to the door.

Cashel said, "Good luck. And remember: I don't know you."

On her way out, Deirdre turned and said, "I wonder, Cashel. Do you know anybody?"

Antrim lay in bed, watching the light come up on her daylight lamp. Slowly, the round sphere that sat on the table at her bedside became brighter and brighter, signaling that it was morning and time to start the day. She preferred it to the loud ping of the wristband alarm which always made her jump. She rolled out of bed and began dressing in the light of the lamp. Grabbing for her wristband, she snapped it on and checked the time.

Hitting her earbud device, she subvocally dictated a tickertape message to Deirdre. The message read, "I need to talk. Where have you been? I need you. Will you meet me in the Wave Room in 20? I'm going for a ride before school."

Deirdre was still wandering the hallways after her meeting with Cashel when the message came in. She read it and wondered what Antrim could need to talk about so early in the day. *Well, that's fine. I have some things of my own to talk about. Like how I'm going to get into the med clinic.*

Back in her room, Antrim grabbed her knapsack out of the closet and gently slid her bedroom door open so she wouldn't wake her Uncle Brandan. She grabbed a Flavor B Nutripak from the cupboard for herself and set out a Flavor D for her uncle. He liked it when she made him breakfast. Slurping down her own, she then went to the bathroom. She quickly washed her teeth and face with antiseptic mist using the pullout wand next to the mirror. Then she grabbed hold of the sink to wait for the predictable post-Nutripak dizziness to pass and examined her hair in the mirror.

Giving it a fluff, she decided she was presentable and headed out the door with her things.

The lift ride to the Wave Room was quite a few levels. But she finally made it to the hallway on Level 40 and entered the area through the double sliding glass doors. A slow grin spread across Antrim's face as she looked out across the open space. She liked to come early before school when the course was empty. It was better than having to vie with the more aggressive kids for space. Quite a few times, Antrim had been elbowed out of a jump to the sound of laughter and jeers. It wasn't fair, but it wasn't really worth a battle, either.

She grabbed her board out of her bag and tossed her knapsack onto the bench. Pulling both ends of it apart, she extended it into the familiar hourglass shape of her skateboard. Antrim looked out across the concrete hills and valleys, high and low shapes forming the waves from which the room got its name. Some city restructure from long ago had warped and bent the concrete, forming the peaks and rolls in the surface. The Minister had allowed the kids to have the space as an exercise area.

Placing her board on the floor, she hopped on. The front edge listed into the air as she balanced all of her weight on the back end. The board was new tech, a rare present from her uncle for her 14th birthday. Its smooth metal surface hovered a few inches off the floor; it could keep her entire body weight suspended for hours before the battery life ran out. It was built to glide with almost zero friction along the bottom by transferring all of the friction to her feet, keeping them solidly planted on the board surface. Next to Deirdre and Flynn, the board was her best friend.

Using a gentle rocking motion, she scooted over to the edge of the first big valley, a 20-foot drop. She felt her heart race and took a long deep breath to steady herself. This was always the best moment, looking down the throat of the great concrete creature and then tipping your weight over the edge in a burst of boldness. She threw herself into the drop and her board hurtled downward, her body almost parallel with the floor. She leaned into the first curve, leveraging her body against gravity with a slingshot trick.

Then she was up the next wall and over Widow's Peak. The nervous voice inside her head stopped and she was all motion. As she hit the peak, the momentum catapulted her upward and she was airborne. Pulling her knees tight against her body, she tapped the front of her board with her palm as she glided through the air. Then, she stretched out again and prepared for a second crouch as her board connected with the concrete. She angled left across the next flat stretch and headed for the Caterpillar. "Today is my 720!"

The Caterpillar was a row of closely spaced peaks, increasing in height and width until they ended at a cliff. Here, riders could get up enough speed to throw themselves into the air, executing a full 360° turn, and land on the opposite cliff. There, a second set of similar peaks were spaced. Many a rider had smacked themselves into the opposite precipice while attempting two 360° turns in a row – the 720.

Antrim had also gotten herself pretty banged up in the past trying to land this trick on the Caterpillar. But today was different. Maybe she felt that her time until Selection was running out. Or maybe it was that Flynn was in trouble and she needed the abandon of the ride. She started out slow on the little hills and gradually built her speed as they became bigger and bigger.

Five hills left.

Three hills left.

One hill left!

On the top of the last peak, she threw her weight hard against the right side of the board, beginning a spin to the right as she ascended into the air. She knew that she needed at least three seconds of airtime to make both turns, and she hoped that she had enough height to do it. As she twisted through the air, she felt her long bangs wrap around her face at the end of the first turn.

"One thousand one," she whispered. Antrim cleared her mind completely and thought of nothing but flying and turning. Not even a thought of Flynn's trouble squeaked in.

"One thousand two." Coming around the second turned, she kept her eyes on the prize – the ledge of the next cliff.

"One thousand three!" She landed it, the board's back edge bumping up and over the ledge from the force of forward momentum. "Yes!" She put two fists into the air and pumped her arms.

Her body coursed with adrenaline as she easily took the smaller peaks on the other side of the Caterpillar. Leaning left into the next turn, she headed to a medium-sized cliff, her favorite handstand spot. Her heart swelling with feeling, she forced her board up the side of the cliff, feeling her victory all the way to her toes. Reaching the top, she put out her palm on the concrete and kicked her legs and board up into the air over her head. The handstand trick felt epic. She paused there for a moment, body completely aloft, savoring her win. Then she heard a voice calling from the entrance to the course.

"Pretty awesome 720, Antrim. You finally did it."

Antrim looked back and smiled. It was Deirdre. She came out of her handstand and jettisoned herself down the cliff wall once more, making her way back to the beginning. She catapulted up the first drop and threw her weight over the edge. Antrim came to a stop where Deirdre waited. Both girls settled themselves on the edge of the cliff, feet dangling over the side.

Antrim exclaimed, "You saw!"

"Of course I saw. Although I wouldn't have believed it if I hadn't."

Antrim playfully punched Deirdre in the arm, and both girls giggled.

Deirdre asked, "So, what's the word?"

Antrim replied, "Where have you been? And tell me what is going on with Flynn."

Deirdre replied, "I'm sorry, Antrim. I was called in by the Ministry for an interview. I had to sit with the top guy in Dream Justice. Again. They've got some issue with a dream Maeve and my mother were working on, and now I'm on the watch list because I downloaded it. I think the interview went alright, but still, I'll need to be careful about where I go and what I do."

Antrim picked up her board and hugged it to her chest. "Oh, Dee. I'm scared. As soon as Flynn was hauled out of school, ticker messages went wild. Is he ok? What's happening?"

Deirdre said in a halting voice, "Flynn messaged me from quarantine. He's in real trouble, and we need to help him."

"But what can we do?"

"They know about his ageing disorder, Antrim. It's bad. The Medical Director wants him scheduled for an early descent. Like, within a few days."

Antrim's face wrinkled up in a tight frown. "Dee, that's wrecked. They can't do that, can they?"

"It will be the Minister's decision. And you can imagine what that means. Flynn doesn't have much time."

Antrim glanced at Deirdre's face and said, "Wait. I can tell you've got something."

"Oh, I do. I'm just going to need you and your new 720 to pull it off."

"If it's skating, I can do it. I know I can."

Deirdre smiled and said, "I know you can too."

The two friends spent the rest of the morning whispering about the plan. In the early afternoon, they decided to case the medical clinic entrance to finalize their attack. Deirdre smiled to herself as they walked past the Drones on guard. Then she turned to Antrim and giggled like they were two Matchers on their way to get their hair and nails done. The Drones never even looked in their direction. *That Medical Director has no idea what we're about to bring on. This will work.*

It was 2:45, and both girls were ready. They huddled together around the corner from the medical clinic and reviewed the final details of their plan. Deirdre pulled Flynn's cloak out of her sack and wrapped herself in it, obscuring her face with the loose edge. She said to Antrim, "Is your board ready?"

"Of course it is," said Antrim, and she bent to pull it out of her knapsack.

"Ok. It's ten minutes 'til the hour. According to the underground, that snitch should be coming out soon. I'm going to take a look around the corner. Stay out of sight." Deirdre leaned around into the intersection and studied the entrance to the clinic up the hall. Then she ducked back out of sight. "Just as before.

Two Drones guarding the entrance, and boxes of medical supplies right next to them. Now you look." Antrim leaned around the corner and studied the setup. Deirdre whispered in her ear, "Can you make it up that stack of boxes for your jump?"

Antrim pulled back and said, "Sure can. But what if I don't get to the lift in time?"

"You'll be long gone before they figure out what happened. Remember, take the lift to the next level up and hide around the corner. They'll they come off the lift after you. Then jump back on when they've moved along. Head home and I'll meet up with you when this is finished. Trust me, ok?" Antrim nodded. Deirdre looked out again and saw the man in the white lab coat leave the clinic, nodding to the Drones on his way out. She turned and gave Antrim a thumbs up.

Antrim extended her board and hopped on. "Give me a push and prepare to be amazed," she said with a wink.

Deirdre pushed off on Antrim's back and sent her sailing down the hallway straight for the boxes and the Drones. Then she leaned out again to follow the action. She shifted her weight from foot to foot, preparing to run. *This has to work. If it doesn't, I don't know what else we can do for Flynn. Fifteen minutes to get this done.*

Antrim kicked off on the concrete floor again and again. Faster and faster she sped, straight for the stack of boxes and hidden from the Drones on the other side. When she reached the base, she threw all of her weight on the back edge of the board, lifting the front into the air. The anti-friction jets connected and she was sent up the side of the stack. The top edge was coming fast, and Antrim went into a half-crouch. With the Drones' heads in view, she slammed down hard on the back left corner of the board. Then she was airborne. She came out of the first 360 and began the second spin. She was sailing straight for their heads. On plan and on schedule she started screaming, "Victory or death!"

The Drones looked up, their eyes immediately shifting to red. But it was too late; Antrim came out of the second turn and crashed into both of them. The two Drones went down in a jumble. Antrim went into a roll and leapt to her feet. Her board had continued down the hallway, and Antrim quickly scanned around for it.

Looking back at the Drones, the redhead said, "Later, jerk weeds," as she took off after her board. In a few long strides, she was on it again. She looked back over her shoulder to make sure the Drones were following. She saw that their eyes were full red and they were after her.

They shouted, "Stop, you're under arrest!" Antrim had a head start for the lift, and she was going to need it. As soon as the Drones sped around the corner, Deirdre started down the hallway and ducked into the medical clinic.

The Medical Director boarded the nearest lift and hit the button for Level 0, Topside. Floor after floor the lift rose, out of the cold concrete of the city. He stepped off and entered a hallway of floor to ceiling glass. The natural light was a little dizzying for eyes accustomed to the low lighting of the underground city. He squinted and took in the view as he walked.

On one side he looked down on the stone courtyard between Dream Justice and the Academy. Makers in their orange robes scurried back and forth, some in pairs and some alone. The damp sea air caught their robes around their ankles and they bent toward each other against the cold gusts. On the other side of the hall, Odran looked out to sea. The unrelenting wind churned the waves into white crests and they beat against the rock of the island. He walked the length of the hall, happily humming a tune as he made ready for Flynn's end.

The doorway at the end was the entrance to the Second's waiting room. A woman in a tight grey dress stood up to welcome him. She said, "Just a moment. I'll see if he's ready for you," and disappeared into Dylan's office. Odran sat down to wait, crossing his legs and staring out to sea.

Ten floors below the Director, Deirdre hesitated in the main hallway of the clinic. It stretched before her, a sterile white corridor with empty exam rooms on all sides. She checked her cloak to make sure her face was hidden and started walking. *You never know when they are watching. And if they are, I'm not giving them any clues about me.* White curtains covered the doorways to the exam rooms and she could see metal exam tables and gurneys where the curtains had been pushed back.

Halfway down the hall, she heard voices coming her way. Deirdre ducked into the nearest exam room and waited for them to pass. Then she peeked out from behind the curtain and saw two men walking away, their huge backs squeezed into two white jackets.

One said, "So. The Director is up meeting with the Second?"

The other said, "Yeah. I can't wait to get rid of that boy."

Deirdre's hand tightened on the curtain. *Flynn!*

"Me too. But I do want to be there when the Director tells him he's headed for the cylinder." Both men gave out a throaty laugh.

"Let's get those boxes brought in and be done with it."

"Naw. Are you kidding? I'm getting out of here to take a break while I can. Come on. Let's catch a few minutes of dream." Then they were out the door, not even noticing that the Drones had left their duty station.

Deirdre stepped back into the main hallway and hurried on her way. The end of the hall opened up on a large room with a workstation and chairs at the center. Multiple cells lined the outside of the room and in one she saw him sitting on the floor. "Flynn," she shouted as she rushed toward the barrier.

Flynn looked up and immediately recognized Deirdre by her eyes and strands of blond hair sticking out from under his cloak. He jumped up and shouted, "Don't come any closer!" Deirdre stopped short, just before the electrostatic wall. He continued, "There's an invisible barrier. You can't touch it. But bloody..." Stumbling over his words, Flynn put one hand to his forehead like he had been struck. "What are you doing here? I told you to stay away!"

Deirdre said, "I'm not letting you die. Now quick, there's no time. Tell me where the Director's desk is."

"No, I'm not telling you anything. You need to get out of here."

"Flynn Brennan, you listen up good. I'm not losing you, so get over it. If you want me to get out, then tell me what I need to know. Because I'm not leaving. I'm not leaving you, ok? Now, spill it," she said, pointing at him.

"Oh, all right. You're impossible. It's over there. The main work table to the left. That's where he sits and accesses the cloud." Flynn nervously ran his hand through his hair as he watched her work.

Deirdre went over to the desk and waved her hand underneath. The holo projection of the login screen and digital keyboard appeared over the desk. She looked back at Flynn and smiled. *Victory or death.*

Topside, the Director followed the woman in the tight grey dress down the hall. She silently ushered him into Dylan's office and then left. The Second was sitting at his desk and didn't bother to look up. Odran took in the three walls of glass and the ocean beyond them, and sat down opposite Dylan. He began, "Thank you for seeing..."

Dylan interrupted him, silently raising a finger in the air. Odran sat in silence for the next few minutes, waiting for the Second to make eye contact.

Finally, Dylan brushed aside the holo screen that had held his attention and said, "Good day, Medical Director. I must admit, I was surprised to get your message. A boy with the worst disease on record for the city, and you are the scientist who discovered it."

Odran said, "We must make an example of him. My recommendation, of course. Announce his condition and he'll be hated all the way to the cylinder by the citizens who are with us. The ruined cannot be allowed to prosper, to drain our resources. And for those against us, this will be a demonstration of the Minister's power. A reminder of his absolute control."

Dylan stared into Odran's light eyes. "It's the cylinder or nothing. Well. Let me see the data. Talking points for the Minister, you know."

Odran logged into the cloud on Dylan's desk and began the transfer of Flynn's records to Dylan's portal.

Deirdre said to Flynn, "Watch this!" She pulled the dragonfly egg out of her pocket and held it up to the portal. Following Cashel's instructions, she leaned down and blew on it gently. The egg began to glow a brighter blue, and the colors reflected on the surface started to shift rapidly. Then it started to expand and unfolded into a shimmering dragonfly with four iridescent wings. The wings started to vibrate and it levitated out of Deirdre's hand. Its luminescent blue eyes began to burn like two blue stars in the night sky.

On the Director's holo screen, the login page disappeared, replaced by the file of Flynn's records. The dragonfly wings beat even faster and it began to execute its programming. Each of Flynn's files were deleted and replaced with the ones Cashel had written.

Soon the dragonfly had done its work, and the login screen returned. For a moment it hovered and Deirdre felt sure that it was looking right at her. Then it started to hum and broke apart in a flash of blue light, disintegrating into metallic dust that drifted to the floor.

Deirdre and Flynn turned to each other and at the same time whispered, "Wow." The beautiful, fragile thing was gone, carried away like a secret on the wind.

Dylan's screen blinked, but it was so fast that neither man noticed. Odran said, "My report is in the file, defining the character of his genetic defect and his status as one of the ruined."

The Second opened the Medical Director's report and read through the first lines of text. Dylan's lips grew tight and he looked up from his screen. "I'm looking at it. And I don't have time for jokes, Odran."

"There is no joke. I serve the Ministry in all things. The boy is ruined."

Dylan said through clenched teeth, "Your...report...states that his lab work is normal. No aging disorder. The watermark header says, 'Dylan is a princess.' But I guess you already knew that, since your signature is on it."

The Director sputtered, starting a few sentences but unable to get a thought out.

"This is not funny, Odran. And I don't have time for this."

Finding his voice, Odran said, "But sir. There has been a mistake."

"The only mistake was me taking time out of my day to see you. Now I want you to get back to your lab, let the boy go, and get back to work. The weavers aren't going to upgrade themselves. Now get out."

Odran cupped his hands together and held them out to the Second. His white lab coat pulled tight against his back. "Let me have him a while longer. I can repeat the tests! Prove to you what I found," said the Director in a high-pitched voice. "He is ruined!"

Dylan stood up from his desk and composed a ticker to his assistant. "Please have the Drones on guard come to my office." He leaned toward Odran, placing two knuckles on the desktop. "The work of your Selection is managing the weaver program. Are you stating on record that you refuse the work of your assignment?" The Drones came in and took up stations on either side of the only exit in the office.

Odran glanced back at the Drones and licked his lips. "No, sir. I will perform my duties as required. The Ministry provides."

Dylan sat down and motioned for the Drones to leave. "Very well, Medical Director. I look forward to your progress on the new

Dream Protocol interface. I want a project plan with deadlines sent to my desk by morning."

The Director stood up and backed out of the room, a beaten man.

Deirdre made a fist and shouted, "Yes!" She turned to Flynn and said, "I think it worked. The Second should be looking at normal lab data right now."

Flynn leaned back against the wall and let out a long exhale. "I can't believe it. You're serious stubborn, but you're amazing."

"Thanks. On both accounts." Deirdre turned back toward the desk to close down the login page. But as she did so, the sleeve of her cloak brushed across the visual keypad.

Flynn raised his arms and shouted, "Stop!" But the damage had been done. Multiple characters had been entered, and each one was automatically submitted to the cloud. Characters that didn't match the Director's password.

The overhead lights switched from white to a blinking red. Deirdre gasped. Alarms echoed through the small space, each one louder than the last. Deirdre whipped back toward Flynn, her face white with terror. He yelled, "You have to run!"

But Deirdre was stuck to the floor, frozen. *Where do I run to? Cashel won't take me in.*

Flynn yelled, "Just get out of here, now!"

Just get going. Figure it out later. Deirdre pulled the cloak up around her knees and forced herself to take the first step. Then another. Then she was off, gaining speed with each stride.

Flynn called after her, "Just get away and FIND SOMEWHERE TO HIDE!"

It was a flat run to the door of the clinic, and Deirdre was fleet footed. But the main hallway of the city was slippery. She lost traction and skidded out, slamming into the opposite wall where more boxes were stacked. Stunned, Deirdre lay motionless on the floor. Everything went into slow motion from the impact.

Through the haze she heard someone screaming her name, sounding as though she was really far away. Deirdre rolled over and looked up the hallway. Blinking hard, she saw two Drones coming back with a struggling, kicking Antrim. The plan hadn't worked, they had caught her anyway. *No, I told her to trust me.* The soldiers were close and coming on fast.

Both Drones paused when they saw Deirdre sprawled on the hallway floor. *Oh no. They're getting orders.* Then the Drones dropped Antrim and took off in her direction.

Antrim screamed, "Run! Run!" Then she took off herself to find a place to hide.

Deirdre scrambled to her feet and sprinted up the hallway in the other direction. The Drones followed close enough that she could see the red light from their eyes reflecting on the floor ahead of her. On through the hallways she ran, looking over her shoulder whenever she felt brave enough.

A Drone shouted, "Stop! You're under arrest!"

Deirdre knew what would happen if she did. Thoughts of Zinna and the horror of dreamlock flashed in her mind. So she ran as hard as she could without skidding out on the painted concrete floor. *If they catch me, I'm done.* She looked over her shoulder again and saw one loading a 'Mare onto his wrist device. He fired just as she turned the corner, the transmission hitting the wall behind her. *Missed!*

Scrambling to get her speed back, she made it to the lift on that section and hit the call button. The location light lit up above the door. *For the love of...the lift is seven floors down. It's not going to make it.* She kicked into gear again, with the Drones now even closer. They fired on her a second time, and this time they hit her square in the head.

Deirdre didn't even look back, she just kept running. She was a girl of 15 with no arachnoid to upload the transmission. But now her disguise was blown.

A Drone shouted, "Arm the locust. She's under 16!"

Around the next corner she ran, praying that the next lift would be on her floor. Behind her, the Drone activated a locust and sent it flying toward her, armed to deliver a 'Mare on contact. Up ahead, the doors to the lift opened; it was the sweetest sound

Deirdre had ever heard. Two people got off and she pushed past them, stumbling through the doors into the tiny compartment.

Luck was with her again; the locust's scanning routine became confused by all the people and attached itself to a woman Deirdre had pushed into its path by accident. She fell to the floor twitching while Deirdre slammed her palm on the 'close door' button. The pistons engaged and the heavy metal doors began to slide shut. Deirdre backed up against the wall of the lift, willing the doors to close with everything she could muster.

Just as they were about to seal, a red-gloved hand thrust itself through the crack. The safety mechanism engaged and the doors slid open again. The space was flooded with red light from the Drones' eyes. *No. No. No!* Standing at the opening were the two Dream Drones with smiles on their faces.

One said, "You're caught, little girl. Very bad for you."

Deirdre looked up at the ceiling and pushed herself as far into the back wall as she could. Her eyes darted left and right but there was nowhere else to run. There were no loose wall panels or ceiling tiles; she was trapped. *How long will I be dreamlocked? How bad will the 'Mare be?*

She closed her eyes as the Drone pulled another locust from out of his belt. This one was bigger than the other and colored a flat brown with a yellow belly. He flung it toward her and it clicked rapidly as it glided through the air. She couldn't watch and turned her head to the wall. The device attached itself to her forehead, just like the other one had done with Flynn. Her eyes rolled back and she collapsed to the floor. The 'Mare had her.

> *Deirdre was falling from a great height. The air was cold and her hair blew up around her like a golden veil. Ice crystals collected in her curls and they turned rigid as she fell. And then she crashed headlong into a body of ice-cold water. The freezing temperature bit into her skin like a thousand pinpricks, and her eyes flew wide open. Above her was the light of the surface, but a powerful current was sucking her down, down, down into the dark. She flailed against the downward pull, kicking with her legs and reaching with her arms. She knew that the single*

breath of air in her lungs wouldn't last much longer. At the last moment, just as she felt that she might open her mouth and drink down the dark water, the riptide from below released her. She kicked for the light, but soon the true horror of the 'Mare became clear. The surface was sealed away with a thick layer of ice and frost. There would be no air for her lungs in this underwater prison. She beat her fists against the ice to no avail; the dark water wouldn't let go. She was drowning with the surface just out of reach.

She tried to scream a curse at the Minister, but in this 'Mare there was only silence. No sounds at all. She sucked down the freezing water and choked, over and over. Mercifully, she passed out. In that brief moment of unconsciousness, a hundred images flickered through her mind, each one like a photograph taken with a magnesium flash bulb. Images of Roenin, Flynn, and the red oak tree kept appearing. In the back of her mind her own voice formed a question: how does Roenin know about the Dream Protocol?

On the surface of the frost, something new came into the dream, something that the 'Mare Makers would never have sequenced. The ice started to hiss and steam. A pattern wrote itself into the ice block; the five-circle symbol of the Makers. It burst into flame, melting the ice and cold all around the Maker's daughter. Deirdre felt her body rising out of the water. In dream, she came Awake.

Deirdre's eyes snapped open. *I'm in the Ritual Room. How long was I out?* She was being dragged across the floor by two Drones holding her wrists. One opened his mouth to speak, and Deirdre quickly shut her eyes before he noticed she was awake.

The Drone said, "Orders are, it's the cylinder for this one. One less problem to deal with."

The other said, "Yeah. Dreamlock in cold storage can only rehabilitate a person so much." They let go of her hands and she let herself flop to the floor like she was still unconscious.

Not the cylinder!

The first Drone said, "You prepare the tube while I notify those below about the unscheduled descent." The soldier walked over to the Cylinder of Descent and exposed the controls inside the wall.

They're going to send me down there if I don't get out of here. Deirdre opened one eye a tiny crack and saw both Drones with their backs turned about ten feet away. Moving slowly and silently, she rolled over onto her stomach and slid up onto all fours. She had lost Flynn's cloak in the struggle, and now she was just in her greys. *Better for running. Here goes.* She darted for the door and ripped the now lifeless locust off of her face. She pushed herself off the doorjamb and into the hallway.

One Drone heard her footsteps and shouted, "Hey! She's getting away!" The Drones set off in pursuit, abandoning the cylinder controls.

The other shouted, "How is she awake? That dreamlock is 60 minutes!"

Deirdre raced down the hall, careening around one intersection after another. The intersections were placed close on Level 48, which gave her the advantage; she was smaller than the Drones and could take the turns a lot faster than them. Soon, she was lost and running through sections she had never seen before. As long as she was moving, she had a chance. But the further she went, the darker it got...the overhead lights flickered or were just completely out.

Behind her the Drone yelled, "Stop! This is a restricted area! Go no farther."

Deirdre ignored him and ran on. Her legs started to hurt and her throat felt dry, but still she ran. The light was so dim she could barely see, so she didn't make out the yellow hazard tape until it was too late. Plastic tape had been strung all across the hallway to warn off anyone from going further, but Deirdre blundered into the tape like a fly into a cobweb. She stumbled and twisted, getting deeper into the strands of adhesive with every step.

She forced herself on with all of her strength, tearing at the tape with her nails. In her struggle, she didn't notice that the flooring had changed from concrete to strips of plywood. The old wood creaked underfoot, but she didn't hear it. The Drones stopped running at the edge of the tape and took on the dazed look of Drones receiving orders.

Deirdre got clear of the tape and looked back, a victorious grin on her face. She said, "Too scared to come and get me?"

Then the flooring gave way and she fell through the splintered boards and into the black, secret depths of the city. Her screams cut off when she hit something hard down below. The Drones turned and walked back the way they had come, as if the events of the last half hour had never happened.

6

Research Findings
Patients ███, ███, and ███ have responded poorly to the first human trials with a surgically placed wireless network node. Surgery went as planned without complications. Nodes were placed under the skin behind the ear and the site was allowed to heal before data transfer. After the first data transfer, all subjects showed signs of ████████ and ██████ behavior. Dr. █████ ordered that the implants be removed. However, all three patients were found dead from ████████████ before the procedure could be reversed.

Executive Action
Remove Dr. ██████ from position as Medical Director. Continue testing implant technology on new volunteers. I am sure Dr. █████ will be happy to participate as a subject. Dispose of the ██████ discrete location.

- Executive Briefing to the Minister of Dream Justice
July 25, 2048

No one came looking for Deirdre because no one knew where to look. When she finally came to, she opened her eyes in a tar-black night. She heard moisture dripping somewhere and there was a musty smell on the air. She tried to move, but her head hurt enough to bring tears to her eyes. She ran her fingers along the back of her head and felt for the sore spot there. Her fingers came away with dried blood. *Where am I? Why can't I see?*

She waved her hand in front of her face, and the motion triggered one weak emergency light bulb. Only a tiny trickle of light penetrated the black. She was in a hallway, with the same concrete flooring that she had lived with her entire life. But instead of walls along the sides, she made out metal scaffolding and rebar, as if the bones of the city were showing through. *But I fell down. Down? What is this place?*

Slowly, she rolled over and pushed herself up on her elbows. She stayed that way for a full minute, waiting for the swimming in her head to stop. Then she willed herself onto all fours and looked toward the light. In her fall, much of the flooring from the level above had come down with her. The path behind her was blocked and she had no choice but to crawl forward. *Wait a minute. Could this be a way to Blue Sky?*

It was cold where she was, the kind of cold that soaks into your muscles and leaches out all the feeling. Deirdre felt along the floor and moved forward until her knee bit into something hard and small. She reached back and grabbed for it. There was a smooth, raised pattern at one end and the bite of something like sharp teeth at the other. Made of a dark yellow metal, it caught the meager light and shimmered like a Maker's amulet. Whatever it was, it was small enough to fit in her pocket, so she put it away and quickly forgot about it.

Moving again, she activated another light from above. She grabbed for the rebar and pulled herself up to a standing position, then continued to feel her way through the corridor. The pale blue light from behind cast a long shadow of her body in front of her. *This level was abandoned a long time ago.* In a city where thousands were crammed into a contained underground space, she had almost never been alone. The isolation of the dark and the crushing quiet was terrifying.

She almost turned around and began the climb out of there – back to what was known. But then she saw it a few feet ahead – the smooth glass of the Cylinder of Descent. It jutted out into the hallway, a half-circle of exposed glass. Curiosity outweighed fear. She stumbled forward, drawn to it by the questions that had always lurked in her mind. *What is really down there?* She placed her palms on the surface just like she had seen Maeve do; and then she peered down inside it. She could see the bottom of the tube lower down, about another level below. *Another level under this one? How many more are there?*

With her movement, another light switched on, and she could see to the end of the hallway. *There is a lift down here!* And that meant there was a way down to where the cylinder ended. Deirdre stared at it for a moment. *Come on, Dee. Don't you want to go and see?* So she forced herself forward, each stumbling step in the decrepit hallway kicking up a small cloud of dust. *I shouldn't be here. But still, I have to know.*

Deirdre felt fear rising again in the back of her throat. She swallowed against it, but the lump remained. She couldn't figure why she suddenly felt so nervous, so she kept going. Behind her, outside the pool of light, something followed her in the dark. Deirdre Callaghan was not alone. Something else was down there with her, awake and alerted by the intrusion into the secret corner of the city. Keeping out of sight, it watched her with two tiny red eyes.

She reached the end of the hallway and hit the call button. As the doors opened, Deirdre jumped back, suddenly realizing that the lift might carry Drones. But, it was empty. She stepped on and the doors slid closed without a sound. There were only three options on the panel inside: Level T, Level 49, and Level 50. *Level T? That's Topside, for the Academy and Dream Justice. A secret lift from the surface to levels that shouldn't exist?*

A tiny antenna popped up on the shiny thing hiding in the shadows and a communication was sent.

Deirdre knew she would meet Drones if she went to the surface; every access point to Topside was guarded. So she selected the button for 49. Nothing happened. *I must already be on Level 49, one level below the Ritual Room.* She whispered in the dark, "What could possibly be on Level 50?" With a slightly trembling hand, Deirdre hit the button for Level 50 and began a descent of her own making.

The ride downward dripped by like time had slowed down. Deirdre could feel her underarms getting wet with sweat. Finally, the lift slowed, stopped, and opened. Remembering her mother's words once more, Deirdre stepped forward. The motion-activated lights in the floor brightened the area as she walked, casting small pools of ghostly light on the ceiling. Deirdre peered down the long hallway before her. Not knowing what was down there made the void seem even darker. She brushed against a wall and recoiled quickly. It was soft and covered with slimy mold; it felt almost like flesh. *Come on, Dee. The walls are not alive. They are just wet from the dank air.*

A far-off sound of whirring and clicking drew her forward. She walked toward the noise, floor lights switching on along her path. The source of the sound was in a large room on her left. She turned into the doorway and stiffened. There sat a hulking machine with eight pairs of arms, and each set of arms held a winter-white Ritual Offering jumper. The arms bobbed and weaved with the kind of speed only a machine can sustain. Using slicing edges and pinching tongs, it quickly picked out the stitches of the jumpers and then wound the loosened yarn into balls. Like some deviant spider, its work was undoing the web of wool yarn; instead of building, it was tearing apart. Each extracted ball of yarn was dropped on a conveyor belt, which then disappeared into the dark section of the room.

Where is the yarn going? Deirdre carefully maneuvered around the spider-like machine, staying away from its churning arms. She walked beside the conveyor belt, following the balls of yarn. More lights switched on with her footsteps. She almost stepped over the ledge when the last light was triggered. Catching herself just in time, Deirdre wobbled precariously on the edge of a cavernous expanse.

In the room before her, the conveyor belt continued into open space, supported by thick tension wires from above. At the center it dropped its winter-white passengers onto a massive pile. The stockpiled yarn balls stretched across the entire room. There were hundreds of them. Thousands. With horror, she realized what this meant: the yarn was being recycled. *No one is going to Tír na nÓg in their jumpers*. The betrayal of sending someone to the next world unmarked by their family pattern was so huge it was almost unthinkable. *But if the yarn is here, then where are all the people? The Ministry must be keeping more than one secret down here.*

She turned and hurried out of the room, past the spider-like machine. Back in the hall, she turned toward the shadowy section of the level and forced herself on, through the dark and the damp. It felt like she was moving down the throat of some great beast; the farther she went, the harder it would be to get out again. *The walls are not alive. This is no beast, just a hallway.*

The corridor widened slightly, and then she saw it again. She knew it by sight immediately; it was the cylinder. *Ok. There it is. But this level is huge. What else is down here?* Its glass door was open, as if someone had just been taken out of it. She quickened her steps to get away from the thing, as if it could somehow reach out and snag her before her time. As yet another light switched on in the floor, a spotlight landed on a map hanging there.

She approached the aging print with faltering steps. It looked old; the paper was yellowed and curling up out of the edges of the frame. Some patches were missing where the fibers had crumbled to dust with the years. The colors were faded, but Deirdre could still make out green for land and blue for water. The map showed a single landmass surrounded by water. At the bottom, the land jutted out in the shape of a hand, and letters in large type were printed there.

In a soft voice, she sounded it out. "Ireee...Land. Ireland?" She ran her fingers across the letters, careful not to cut herself on the broken glass that still clung to the frame. *This is important. It must be. Ireland. But what does it mean?* There were a handful of red dots sprinkled across the landmass, but she was drawn to the largest one. The dot looked like it was out in the water. Her fingers drifted over to touch it. "No, not in the water. There's an island there. Skellig Michael." *Like Skellig City?* At the bottom of the frame was a tarnished brass plate that read 'IDream Holdings 2547.'

Then she heard a voice. "C'mere," someone hissed. "Everyone. Everyone. They're coming. Shh! Shh!"

Deirdre turned and crept down the corridor toward the sound. *Are they Ministry or someone else?* Soon she could make out row after row of rusting metal bars. She thought at first the bars were just more scaffolding, but she soon discovered the truth. The bars formed cells with doors and locks on them. Then she heard more voices drifting through the hallway and it hit her. *The ruined. They're still here! No one is in Tír na nÓg!* She ran to the nearest cell, put her hands on the bars, and pressed her face into the space between them. She called out, "Who's there? Is there someone in there?"

As her eyes adjusted to the darkness in the cage, she saw four people cowering against the back wall. They were dressed only in their underclothes. "Everyone relax," said a man. "It's not a Dream Drone. It's one of us." The prisoners rushed to her, grasping at her hands. All of them spoke at once, pushing their own faces between the bars.

One said, "How did you get here, child?"

Another said, "Were there any Dream Drones out there?"

Still another asked, "Can you get the door open?"

"Just one sec. Let me try." Deirdre tugged at the door with all her strength, but the deadlock kept it tight. Frantically, she looked around for some way to open it, something she could use as a lever against the lock. She ran back to the map and pulled at a section of wood frame. But it was so old that it disintegrated to splinters in her hand. She said, "I'm sorry. I don't have anything to get it open." It was then that she heard another voice farther down the hallway.

"Deirdre? Deirdre, is that you?"

The voice sounded so familiar, a memory bubble bursting to the surface. Breaking away from the cries in front of her, Deirdre ran for the other voice, one frantic footstep placed in front of the other. "Maeve," she called. "Is that you? Are you there?"

Maeve called back, "Here, Deirdre! I'm here."

Reaching her cell, Deirdre reached inside the bars to embrace her old friend. "Maeve, I can't believe it's you. I thought you were gone forever."

"Child!" Maeve said. "What are you doing here? How did you find us?"

Maeve felt weak and thin. Deirdre said, "I was helping Flynn escape an early descent. But the Drones found me and chased me through Level 48. Then I fell through the floor and woke up here. I don't even know how much time has passed. What is this place? What is happening here?"

Maeve gently reached out through the bars and wiped away a single tear that had fallen onto Deirdre's cheek. Softly, she replied, "Dear one. If only I knew. This place is a prison."

"But I don't understand. You are all supposed to be on your way to Tír na nÓg."

Maeve said, "When I reached the bottom of the cylinder, two Dream Drones stripped me of my jumper and threw me into this cell. The man in the cell next to me has been here a month. When we were sure that we weren't being watched, he told me what he had learned. He said there is a train at the end of this corridor, and that all the people held here were herded onto it by the Drones a few weeks past. But there were too many people and he couldn't fit on, so the Drones put him back into the cell and the train left without him."

Deirdre exclaimed, "A train left? Going where? We're on an island!" She took off running down the hallway.

Maeve called after her, "Dee, wait! Come back, lass! Go no closer to that cursed contraption!"

But Deirdre had to see the train for herself. Running hard with lights activating with every step, she found the train at the end of the hall. A yawning space narrowed into a tunnel, which continued off into the black unknown. She paused to take in this extraordinary scene: a train at the bottom of a city in the middle of an ocean. She pinched herself to make sure she wasn't in dream and went closer. The loading platform and the train cars were empty. The train was old; the car numbers barely visible from where the paint had flaked off from the years - maybe centuries.

She stepped up to an open car and boarded. The inside of the car was lined with rusted shackles. As Deirdre looked at them more closely, she saw that the red stains weren't rust - they were dried blood. She shivered. Deirdre backed up, and tripped over one of the chains lying on the floor in her haste. *I could get trapped here so easily.* She lurched up, stumbling off the train and back on the platform.

Then she took a long look down the dark tunnel. Somehow, she felt that it was calling her, a whisper on the close air. *This is not a train to Tír na nÓg.* She thought the sound of her heart pounding in her chest would fill the entire level. *Thump. Thump. Thump.* The bitter smell of fear-soaked sweat filled her nose. *It doesn't matter. I have to know what is down there.*

But at that instant, the loud buzzing of an alarm cut through the tomblike silence of the place. She looked toward the cylinder. *It will bring the Drones. The level will be filled with them any moment!* She turned and ran back up the corridor to the prisoners. Sore as she was, she sprinted back to Maeve's cell and yanked on the unyielding door with all her strength.

She shouted, "Maeve, I have to get you out of here!"

"No, lass. No!" Maeve said. "The Drones will be here any second. It's Siobhan's time any minute now so they probably have a head start. You must get yourself out of here. Flee this place now!"

Deirdre looked into Maeve's eyes as panic filled her.
Mother.

Deirdre wailed, "No! She'll be trapped down here like the rest of you! I have to stop her." She turned away from Maeve to run, and then added, "I promise I'll be back. I promise, you hear?" Then she took off at a sprint again.

Maeve shouted, "Go, child. Go! *Red Oak*, Deirdre. Remember *Red Oak*!" Then Maeve turned to the other prisoners and said, "They'll be coming out of that lift any minute. Everyone please help her! Make as much noise as you can to distract the Drones!"

Darting down the hall for the lift, Deirdre's escape was abruptly blocked. Lights over the lift indicated that it was moving from Level T to Level 50. She skidded to a stop. Someone had called it Topside, and now it was coming back down. She ducked into the yarn room just as the door opened and two Dream Drones stepped off.

One said, "Check the Great Spider first. I'll head down to the prisoner section." The other Drone nodded and walked toward the room where Deirdre hid.

Oh no. They're coming this way! Deirdre took in a deep breath and held it tightly.

But further down the corridor, the cells exploded in noise; the prisoners had taken up Maeve's call and they filled the hallway with their screams and yells. The other Drone said, "No, I'm coming with you first. Something is going on with those ruined." Both soldiers ran past, shouting to the prisoners to quiet down. When they reached the prisoner area, they unlocked one of the cages and grabbed for a man there.

Deirdre forced herself to exhale slowly. *I need to make a run for it now.* Then she sucked in as much air as her lungs could hold and threw herself into the hall. Her feet hit the corridor at a dead run. *Don't look back.* The lift doors were still open. *Ten feet more and I'm there.* Her feet ate up the concrete and her arms pumped in time with her breath.

Her speed slammed her into the back wall of the small chamber. She whirled around and looked at the level options. The Drones hadn't looked her way. *Could I get Topside if I tried? No, I'd be caught and then no one would be there to stop mother's descent.* So she hit the button for Level 49. The doors slid shut just as the Dream Drones wrestled the man out of his cage. *I'll have to get out the way I came in. Please let me get to the Ritual Room in time.*

She shifted back and forth on her feet, restless for the lift to finally slow. *What's the plan?* She would have to find a way up the wall where she had fallen through. The doors opened and she flew out of them, a girl on fire. Past the cylinder she dashed until she came to the section that was blocked with debris. She looked around under the hole above and found scaffolding on one side where wall should have been. With trembling fingers, she searched for a handhold and began to climb fast and true.

Reach. Step. Pull.

Reach. Step. Pull.

Her arms burned from lifting her weight. *What am I going to do when I get to the Ritual Room? The Minister and his Drones will be there. Somehow I've got to get her out of the cylinder.*

Reach. Step. SLIP!

Her feet slipped off of the rusty frame, and she found herself dangling in midair. *Come on, girl. Don't fail Ma. Slow and steady wins the race.* Deirdre took a deep breath, calmed her mind, and felt for the elusive rung with her feet. *Found it.* With careful steps, she climbed up the rest of the way to Level 48.

At the top of the scaffolding, her exit was blocked by the floorboards above. She reached out toward the hole in the flooring but it was just out of reach. *If this flooring is rotten, maybe I can punch my way through.* So she climbed up as far as she could go and wedged her shoulders against the old wood planks. Then she pushed off the rebar against the floorboards, trying to open a new exit. The old wood creaked and groaned, but it held fast. Dust fell down into her face and she started to cough. Again she pushed, and again, until finally the planks broke free and she was through, pulling herself through the splinters.

Up and out she climbed, bursting onto Level 48. She flew through the hallways like a banshee. *I'm close now. So close.* Back into known territory she ran, the lights getting brighter with each intersection. She was tired, dehydrated, and hungry. Still she ran, forcing the speed from her legs, trying to reach her mother in time. But when she rounded the next corner, there was a new wall blocking her route.

"No!" she yelled, slamming both fists into the wall. *Restack!* For a moment, she crumbled, tears of frustration squeezing out of her closed eyes. *I'm so tired.* And then her memory flashed on all of the ruined being held against their will on Level 50. Where they had planned to put Flynn. So, she wiped her eyes and found the information panel in the wall. Bringing up the new crowd flow pattern for Level 48, she realized that she was going to have to run all the way around the exterior wall of the city to reach the Ritual Room. *Blast it.*

Her mouth was parched and her throat was dry. But still she willed a jog from her legs. The deep gulps of air she took pained her throat even more. *Minister! If I ever get the chance, I'd trade it all just to wring your neck.* She made it the length of one section and then ran on to the next. *Mother, are you in the cylinder yet?* Another section passed by. The muscles in her legs burned from lack of oxygen. *Don't go in there, Ma!*

She was almost there. The people arriving for the ritual looked on surprised as the daughter of the ruined sped through the hallways. But outside the entrance, she crashed headlong into a Drone. Its eyes flashed red and it demanded an explanation.

Deirdre stammered, "Oh. Um. I'm sorry. It's my mother's descent. I'm going to miss it." Then she choked out, "The Ministry provides." Its eyes went dim once again and she was released.

The Ritual Room was filled with the sound of chanting and a drum beat. As Deirdre entered she heard the last wish was being offered, and she was just in time to see the large glass door shut over her mother. Screaming, she pushed her way through the crowd. Her long golden hair whipped back and forth as she fought through the layers of bodies.

"Ma! Stop! Don't go down there! Please!" She broke through the last row of people and rushed to the dais, pressing her face and hands against the Cylinder of Descent.

The timer chimed thirty seconds left.

Siobhan yelled back, trying to make her voice heard through the thick clear glass. "Daughter. Hush now! Be still."

"Oh, Ma," she wailed. "I'm too late. I'm so sorry." Tears streamed down her face. "Ma! Ma, get out of there. Don't go. Listen to me...there are..."

Breck was standing in the front row with her father, and she stepped out of line and pointed at Deirdre, shouting, "C'mere! Stop it, Deirdre. There are rules. This is Ma's special moment, and you're spoiling it!"

The timer hit 10 seconds left.

Siobhan placed one palm on the glass atop Deirdre's trembling hand. "Deirdre," she said. "None of that, now. You must be strong. I have accepted my fate." Her words started coming faster. "Quickly now, there isn't much time. There's something I must leave you with about *Red Oak* and your father..." The last alarm sounded and the flooring opened up below her. With a rush of air, Siobhan was gone.

Deirdre collapsed to the floor, screaming her mother's name. The Minister commanded the two Drones on guard for the ritual to pick her up. His voice brought order to the room.

"Get her out of here," he said. "The Ministry provides. Today we make the gift of an exception for the Ritual Offering's daughter. Let no one say that the Ministry is not merciful."

Deirdre allowed herself to be carried from the room by the Drones as her father stood stoically at the front of the crowd. He hadn't moved through the whole thing. The Dream Drones deposited her on the hallway floor outside the Ritual Room and walked away to escort the Minister. Deirdre felt empty. Like she had nothing left. *I failed. She's gone.*

Then she heard a familiar voice. "Dee? Dee? What happened? Are you all right?"

She felt a gentle hand lifting her chin and saw that it was Flynn who was calling to her. Wrapped in a new cloak, he let the cloth fall away from his face.

Deirdre grabbed hold of him. "Flynn! You're OK! But I'm too late," she sobbed. "Ma is gone. Taken."

Flynn put a hand on the side of her face. "Yes, I'm alright – thanks to you. By order of the Second. But Deirdre...of course she's gone. I know you're serious wrecked, but this is the day of her descent."

Deirdre clutched at his hand. "No, Flynn. Today...the things I've seen..." She stopped. "Wait, wait, we can go back. We can save her." She struggled to her feet and grabbed Flynn's hand. She pulled him along with her, as fast as he could go through the crowd of exiting people. As they ran through the corridors, Deirdre explained all that had just happened.

Flynn said, "Dee, I don't know what you are talking about. Did something go wrong with one of your dream downloads? There is no level below this one."

Deirdre said, "But I was there, Flynn! And Maeve was there. I talked to her. And that's where Ma is going right now. And we're going after her."

But when they wound their way to the back passageways of Level 48, they hit a wall. There was no way around it; all of the intersections were blocked. Deirdre frantically felt up and down for any crevice that would let them through, but there was nothing. It was as if the entire section of hallway had been rebuilt while she was in the Ritual Room.

"This is impossible. It was right here," she said. "And all those people are down there...being put on a train to who knows where! I swear to you Flynn, they're not going to Tír na nÓg." She started banging on the wall and shouting, "Let me in. Let me in!"

Flynn wrapped his arms around her and pulled her into a tight embrace. "Dee," he whispered, "We have to be smart about this. I don't understand what is happening. But if you say that you saw people at the bottom of the city being held in cages, then I believe you. Maybe we won't figure it out today, but we will figure out what is going on. And when we do, the Ministry will have us to deal with."

She turned in his arms and pulled back just far enough to look into his eyes. "We have to fight them, Flynn. With every weapon we can find. And we have to find my mother. Promise," she implored, gazing up at him with fresh tears falling.

"Promise," he said, and he touched his forehead to hers.

Then she whispered, "There's something I haven't told you yet. My mother and Maeve sent someone to help us. His name is Roenin."

Still with his eyes closed, Flynn said, "Good. We're going to need all the allies we can find. And Dee. There's something I haven't told you." Then he opened his eyes, looked into hers and said, "You asked me what I wanted when we find Blue Sky. All I want is to be with you. I don't care what's out there. As long as we're together." He pulled her into a close embrace.

Deep down on the hidden levels, the walls of the great city rumbled with laughter. A warm, moist wind blew through the hallways of Level 49, almost as if the breath of some great creature was being exhaled. And this wind, as it blew, took on the quality of a metallic voice. "Deirdre Callaghan. At last, fortune blooms like a flower. How long it has been since I was surprised?" the voice mused to itself. On the level below, even the Great Spider attacked its work on the ritual jumpers more joyfully.

In the upper levels of the city, a man in a white lab coat sat at his desk. The holo screen played the recording of Flynn in the quarantine room on the day of his audience with the Second. He watched Flynn pace, lay down, and pace some more. Then the screen went blank. The Director reloaded the file from the cloud archive, but again it went dark. Twelve minutes were missing from the file. "That's impossible," he whispered to himself. "The archive is a perfect record."

He started the recording again, this time from the moment Flynn was brought into the clinic. There was something strange about the boy's behavior, the way he hid his face when resting. He brought up the records for all holo calls logged by Flynn Brennan in the last month. Seeing the info stamps, his face turned red. He hissed, "Deirdre Callaghan. You are going to be sorry. Not this day...but soon. I swear it."

Acknowledgements

First I would like to thank my husband Patrick for all of his support, in big ways and small. You inspired me to write, even when all I had going for me was one tiny idea.

I would also like to think my Dad, F.T. Flynn, who was always excited about my story and just kept asking, "When is it coming out?"

Also I would like to thank my niece Deirdre for being my favorite beta dreamer.

Lastly I would like to thank other authors who have gone before me and who gave me wonderful worlds to explore in their writing.

Adara Flynn Quick

has been an artist, psychotherapist, college professor, hair salon receptionist, house painter, and a dreadful waitress. Early in her career, Adara was fascinated by dreams, the unconscious, and the healing stories of many cultures. She now uses her background as a psychotherapist to create stories of triumph and transformation.

Her stories bring ancient myths and legends into futuristic worlds. Driven to distraction by her computer, Adara writes all of her stories longhand. Pen and paper are two of her favorite things. She resides in the Washington, D.C. area with her husband.

Visit her online at:
www.adaraquick.com

Connect on Facebook to receive author alerts
and learn more about the world of the Dream Protocol:
https://www.facebook.com/AdaraQuick
https://www.facebook.com/TheDreamProtocol

Find Adara Quick on www.Goodreads.com for book reviews and
recommendations.

DEIRDRE CALLAGHAN BELIEVED THAT THE MINISTER OF
DREAM JUSTICE WAS HER GREATEST ENEMY.
SHE WAS WRONG.

Coming Winter 2016
The Dream Protocol: Selection
Copyright © 2016 Adara Flynn Quick

I open my eyes to find myself lying on a medical exam table. I look around and see the Selection Room empty of everyone, even Drones and medical personnel. I must have nodded off. I wonder where everyone is. I swing my legs over the side of the table and land lightly on the floor. That wasn't so bad; I didn't even feel the arachnoid. Maybe I can sneak out of here before anyone notices.

Stealing out of the exam room, I make my way down the long hallway, looking for an exit or someone to show the way out. I finally come to a door with the letters EXIT over the top. Almost to freedom. I throw my weight on the latch, but it won't give. Another hard push, and it finally pops open. I stumble through, slightly off balance.

Righting myself, my eyes are drawn to the only spot of light in the dark room. What I see there makes me freeze. All the moisture dries up in my throat. Deirdre and Antrim are strapped down to two chairs in the center of the room. Both of them are slumped over, their bodies held tight by straps on their neck, arms, and ankles. Why aren't they moving? The spotlight overhead casts a ghostly light that multiplies into contorted human shadows on the floor. It is as silent as midnight in winter.

I rush forward to unbind them, but I run straight into a force field and it holds me a few feet away. I travel in a circle around the barrier feeling along the edge of the field with my fingers, looking for any weaknesses. But I find nothing, and end up back where I started. Desperate, I call out, "Dee! Antrim!"

"They can't hear you," booms a voice that seems to come from everywhere at once.

I jump at the sound and whirl around. "Who's there?" I call, looking frantically into the darkness.

"Why Flynn, I am Skellig City," the voice hisses.

COOKS AND CROOKS TRADE BLOWS IN A DECAYING METROPOLIS, RAVAGED BY HARD TIMES AND CONNIVING POLITICIANS.

It was a typical run-down hard-luck town, common in its own way. People called it the Charmed City, or simply Adversity, depending on their prospects. Like all places where men congregate for generations, it had built a history of itself that was both rich and twisted by the weight of years. It had seen tales of crafty kings of commerce and elegant matrons of culture, as well as the more entertaining and scandalous escapades of depraved, infamous villains, of whom there were many.

The promise of prosperity brought all manner of men, with all their passions and failings. It is said that the riches of Adversity also attracted another sort of beast, a fell creature of avenging conscience drawn to the city by the evil that took root there. It was a fanciful story, but strangely the residents gave it much heed in later days as the city crumbled around them.

The Charmed City was like so many others in this modern age, struggling against the fetters of its past. It had blossomed during the advent of industry with a glut of factories and railroads and feats of mechanical ingenuity. The period of plenty produced a sense of grandeur and complacency that ultimately proved disastrous. The city was not prepared for the lean times that followed. The world changed. Markets tumbled as debts came due and the extravagant promise of boundless economic growth proved false. The city's prosperity faded, unable to keep pace with the times, its wealth draining away into the pockets of crooked politicians and cutthroat capitalists while the citizens watched their waning glory with weary eyes.

In the midst of this chaos, Colonel Dashenka Ivanovna Stavrogin and her men came to town on assignment from the Internal Revenue Service. The country's capital was in dire financial straits, scouring every avenue to avoid utter economic collapse. As such, the collection of the tithe in a fastidious manner became a matter of desperate importance. The Chief Auditor of Adversity was well known for a whimsical sense of arithmetic when it came to balancing the books, so the federal officials had deemed it time for the decennial city audit. Colonel Stavrogin was sent by the Capital with special dispensation to mete out fiscal justice upon the local government with extreme prejudice.

Dashenka was an orderly woman, of definite opinions and a discerning nature. She despised the weakness and depravity of Adversity, but her family had served the I.R.S. for three generations and she was faithful to that legacy. Her lieutenants, Injal Skube and Killer Hrapp, were newly minted immigrants from the north, raised to respect authority and revel in violence. They were loyal as kin to their Colonel, impressed with her fine words and fearful of her ardent will. The three of them burst into town like a cleansing deluge, cracking down on the grifters and penny pinchers and tax fraud gangs.

Their arrival harkened ill days ahead, for there were few in the crumbling metropolis that didn't have some hand in the illicit business of dodging the taxman. The city was generally resistant to the demands of the Capital, caught up in nostalgic longing for its glorious past when it had been a center of culture and the Capital little more than a backwater borough of no standing. The mood had always been one of rakish abandon, but desperation had set in of late. The newcomers suffered interludes of violence to be certain, knives in the night, but the Colonel kept these attacks as quiet as she could out of a sense of propriety – and more importantly, to avoid fomenting more ill will among the disaffected and dissolute populace.

There was another cause for concern in the Charmed City in those final days. Coincident with Colonel Stavrogin's arrival, strange deaths were being reported: bodies found in a horrific state, victims of abominable inhuman violence. Some at first blamed the local crime lord, referred to fancifully as the Princess of Darkness. Others eyed the new arrivals from the Capital with their brutal demeanor. But all soon reached an unspoken consensus the deaths were the work of a creature far older and more foul.

Rumors spoke of roving bands of wild dogs possessed, for tradition held the animals had always been thrall to the city's fell beast. The stories described gruesome gatherings on the West Side of the city where the creature was said to keep its lair, a slum left abandoned save by the most desperate or destitute. Such portents of catastrophe became common talk as the days grew dim.

The storm stirred up by Colonel Stavrogin's arrival was soon to break mercilessly upon the Charmed City. All were hard pressed to withstand the bleak days that followed. Some unwary few found themselves caught directly in the epicenter of events, either by design or unfortunate circumstance. By their frantic efforts, these hapless folk proved pivotal in the tragedy that followed.